LOST IN THE FOREST

R.M. BALLANTYNE

Frontispiece by John Betancourt. Based on a painting.

LOST IN THE FOREST

R.M. Ballantyne

WILDSIDE PRESS

LOST IN THE FOREST

INTRODUCTION

Robert Michael Ballantyne (1825–1894) was a Scottish author who published more than 100 books. He was also an accomplished artist and exhibited some of his water-colours at the Royal Scottish Academy.

Ballantyne was born in Edinburgh, the ninth of ten children (and the youngest son), to Alexander and Anne Ballantyne. His father was a newspaper editor and printer in the family firm of "Ballantyne & Co" based at Paul's Works on the Canongate. His uncle, James Ballantyne, was the printer for Scottish author Sir Walter Scott. A banking crisis in 1825 resulted in the collapse of the Ballantyne printing business the following year with debts of £130,000,which led to a decline in the family's fortunes.

Robert Ballantyne went to Canada at the age of 16 and spent five years working for the Hudson's Bay Company. He traded with the local Native Americans for furs, which required him to travel by canoe and sleigh to the areas occupied by the modern-day provinces of Manitoba, Ontario, and Quebec—experiences that formed the basis of his novel *Snowflakes and Sunbeams* (1856). His longing for family and home during that period impressed him to start writing letters to his mother. Ballantyne recalled in his autobiographical *Personal Reminiscences in Book Making* (1893) that "To this long-letter writing I attribute whatever small amount of facility in composition I may have acquired."

In 1847 Ballantyne returned to Scotland to discover that his father had died. He published his first book the following year, *Hudson's Bay: or, Life in the Wilds of North America*, and for some time was employed by the publishers Messrs Constable. In 1856 he gave up business to focus on his literary career and began the series of adventure stories for the young with which his name is popularly associated.

The Young Fur-Traders (1856), *The Coral Island* (1857), *The World of Ice* (1859), *Ungava: a Tale of Eskimo Land* (1857), *The Dog*

Crusoe (1860), *The Lighthouse* (1865), *Fighting the Whales* (1866), *Deep Down* (1868), *The Pirate City* (1874), *Erling the Bold* (1869), *The Settler and the Savage* (1877), and more than 100 other books followed in regular succession, his rule being to write as far as possible from personal knowledge of the scenes he described. *The Gorilla Hunters: A tale of the wilds of Africa* (1861) shares three characters with The Coral Island: Jack Martin, Ralph Rover and Peterkin Gay. Here Ballantyne relied factually on Paul du Chaillu's Exploration in Equatorial Guinea, which had appeared early in the same year.

The Coral Island remains the most popular of the Ballantyne novels still read and remembered today, but because of a mistake he made in that book—he gave an incorrect thickness of coconut shells—he prioritized research on his subjects for later books. For instance, he spent time living with the lighthouse keepers at the Bell Rock before writing *The Lighthouse*, and he spent time with the tin miners of Cornwall while researching *Deep Down*.

In 1866 he married Jane Grant, with whom he had three sons and three daughters. He spent his later years in Harrow, London, before moving to Italy for the sake of his health, possibly suffering from undiagnosed Ménière's disease. He died in Rome in 1894 and was buried in the Protestant Cemetery there.

One of the young men influenced by Ballantyne's novels was Robert Louis Stevenson (1850–94). Stevenson was so impressed with the story of *The Coral Island* (1857) that he based portions of his most famous book, *Treasure Island* (1881), on themes found in Ballantyne's classic novel.

—Karl Wurf
Rockville, Maryland

CHAPTER I.

At Sea — An Alarming Cry and a Rescue.

"At sea once more!" said Will Osten in a meditative mood.

Our hero made this remark one night to himself, which was overheard and replied to by his friend, Captain Dall, in a manner that surprised him.

"It's my opinion, doctor," said the captain in a low voice, "that this is the last time you or I will ever be at sea, or anywhere else, if our skipper don't look better after his men, for a more rascally crew I never set eyes on, and, from a word or two I have heard dropped now and then, I feel sure some mischief is in the wind. Come aft with me to a place where we ain't so likely to be overheard by eavesdroppers, and I'll tell you all about it."

Will Osten was so much astonished at his friend's remark, that he followed him to the after part of the ship without uttering a word, and there sat down on the taffrail to listen to what he had to communicate.

There was no moon in the clear sky, and the hosts of stars that studded the dark vault overhead did not shed any appreciable light on the waters of the Pacific, on which the *Rover* floated almost motionless. That beautiful and mysterious phosphorescence which sometimes illumines the sea was gleaming in vivid flashes in the vessel's wake, and a glowing trail of it appeared to follow the rudder like a serpent of lambent fire.

It was one of those calm, peaceful nights in which God seems to draw nearer than usual to the souls of His creatures. The only sounds that broke the profound stillness were the pattering of reef-points on the sails as the vessel rose and sank gently on the oily swell; the measured tread of the officer of the watch, and the humming of the man at the wheel, as he stood idly at his post, for the vessel had scarcely steering-way.

"Doctor," said Captain Dall in a low whisper, taking Will Osten by the button-hole and bending forward until his eyes were close to those of his young friend, "I little thought when I set sail from England that, in a few weeks after, my good ship the *Foam* would come a wreck an' sink to the bottom of the Pacific before my eyes. Still less did I think that I should be cast on a coral island, have to fight like a naked savage, and be saved at last by missionaries from being roasted and eaten. Yet all this has happened within a few months."

At any other time Will Osten would have smiled at the solemn manner in which this was said, but there was something in the hour, and also in the tone of his friend's voice, which tended to repress levity and raise a feeling of anxiety in his mind.

"Well, captain," he said, "what has this to do with the present evil that you seem to apprehend?"

"To do with it, lad? nothing — 'xcept that it reminds me that we little know what is in store for us. Here are we becalmed — three day's sail from the coral island, where the niggers were so near converting us into cooked victuals, and I wouldn't at this minute give twopence in security for the life of any one on board the *Rover*."

"Why, what mean you?" asked Will, with increasing perplexity. "Some of the crew are bad enough, no doubt, but many of them are evidently good men — what is it that you fear?"

"Fear! why, there's everything to fear," said the captain in a suppressed but excited whisper, drawing still closer to his friend. "I've often sailed in these seas, and I know that while some of the traders sailing between these islands and South America and other parts are decentish enough, others are as great cut-throats as ever deserved to swing at the yard-arm. But that's not the point. I have overheard, of late, some of the rascals plotting to murder the officers and take this ship. But I cannot point 'em out, for though I heard their voices I couldn't see their faces. I think I know who they are, but could not swear to 'em, and it would be worse than useless to denounce them till we have some evidence to go on. I therefore want you to help me with your advice and assistance, so that we may get up a counterplot to spoil their fun — for I'm quite certain that if we fail to — hark! what's that?"

Will did not answer, but both listened intently to the sound which had interrupted Captain Dall's discourse. It was evident that the officer and men of the watch had also heard it, for they, too, had ceased to walk to and fro, and their figures could be dimly seen in a listening attitude at the gangway.

For several minutes they listened without hearing anything — then a hoarse, guttural shout broke the stillness of the night for a few seconds and died away. The men looked at each other, and some of the more superstitious among them grew pale. Again the cry was repeated, somewhat nearer, and again all was still. Some of the oldest hands in the watch stood transfixed and powerless with terror. They would have faced death in any form manfully, but this mysterious sound unnerved them!

The officer of the watch went down to report it to Captain Blathers, who immediately came on deck. Just as he appeared, the cry was repeated and a slight splash was heard.

"Some one in distress," cried Captain Blathers promptly; "a crew for the starboard quarter-boat to pick him up. Stand by to lower. Be smart, lads!"

These words, heartily uttered, put superstitious fears to flight at once. The men threw off their jackets; the boat was lowered, and in a few minutes was pulling about and searching in all directions. Our hero was one of the first to leap into her, and he pulled the bow oar. For some time they rowed about in vain. The night was intensely dark, and the cry was not repeated, so that they had nothing to guide them in their movements. A lantern was fixed in the ship half way up the mizzen rigging, but the lantern in the boat was concealed until the moment when it should be required, because it is easier for men to distinguish surrounding objects in comparative darkness than when a light is glaring near them. Presently Will Osten saw a dark object like a small canoe right ahead of the boat.

"Back water — all!" he shouted.

The men obeyed, but it was too late; the boat struck the object and overturned it. Will saw something like a human form roll into the water and heard a gurgling cry. Without a moment's hesitation he leaped overboard, head foremost, and catching hold of the object, brought it to the surface. He remembered at that moment having heard of a fact which is worth stating here. The best way to save a drowning man is to approach him from behind, seize him under the armpits, and, then, getting on your back, draw him partly on to your breast and swim *on your back* to the shore, or to a place of safety. Thought is quicker than the lightning flash. Will could not, of course, carry out this plan fully, nevertheless the memory of it served him in good stead, for, the instant he caught the drowning man by the hair, he kept him at arm's length, and thus avoided his death-clutch until he could grasp him under the armpits *from behind*, and thus render him powerless. He then rose and drew him gently upon his breast, at the same time striking out with his feet and shouting —

"Bear a hand, lads — I've got him!"

A loud "hurrah!" burst from the men in the boat, and was re-echoed vehemently from the ship. They had overshot the spot only by a few yards. Instantly they pulled round: two strokes brought them to the spot where Will was swimming, and in another moment our hero and the rescued man were hauled into the boat. The men gave vent to another loud and prolonged cheer, which was again replied to from the ship.

The boat was soon alongside, and the rescued man, who proved to be a man of colour in a very emaciated and exhausted condition, was hoisted on board. His story was soon told. He was not a native of the islands, but had been living on one of them, and had gone off to fish in a canoe, when a gale sprang up and blew him out to sea. Four days and nights had he been exposed to the storm in his frail bark, without food or water, and was on the point of perishing when the ship chanced to pass near him. The utterance of the cry which had attracted attention was almost the last effort of which he was capable. He spoke a little broken English, having learnt it while serving on board of an English trading vessel. His name, he said, was Bunco, and a fine powerful-looking fellow he was, despite the sad condition to which he had been reduced. His shoulders, and indeed most parts of his body, were blistered by the continual washing of the sea over him, and when he was lifted on board his skin was icy cold. Had he not been a man of iron mould, he must certainly have perished. The poor fellow was at once taken into the cabin and carefully attended to. He was first bathed in fresh water, then rolled in blankets, and a tumbler of hot wine and water administered, which greatly revived him, and soon caused him to fall into a sound sleep.

Whether it was that this incident softened the hearts of the seamen for a time, or that their plans were not yet ripe for execution, we cannot tell, but certain it is that nothing whatever occurred to justify Captain Dall's suspicions for several weeks after that.

CHAPTER II.

Describes a Mutiny, and shows that the Best of Friends may part sooner than they expect.

"A wilful man will have his way." That this is a true proverb is almost universally admitted; indeed, there is reason to believe that it is equally true of women as of men; nevertheless, Captain Blathers did not believe it although he was himself a living illustration of its truth. He laughed at Captain Dall when that worthy warned him of the mutinous intentions of his crew, and when several weeks had passed away without any signs of disaffection appearing, he rallied him a good deal about what he styled his suspicious disposition, and refused to take any steps to guard against surprise. The consequence was, that when the storm did break, he was utterly unprepared to meet it.

Griffin, the second mate, was the leader of the conspiracy, but so ably did he act his villainous part, that no one suspected him. He was a tall, powerful, swarthy man, with a handsome but forbidding countenance.

One evening a little before sunset, while the captain was sitting at tea with those who usually messed in the cabin, Griffin looked down the skylight and reported "a sail on the weather bow." The captain immediately rose and went on deck. The moment he appeared he was seized by Griffin. Captain Blathers was an active and powerful man, and very passionate. He clenched his fist and struck the second mate a blow on the chest, which caused him to stagger back, but, before he could repeat it, two sailors seized him from behind and held him fast. The noise of the scuffle at once brought up the first mate, who was followed by Will Osten, Captain Dall, and others, all of whom were seized by the crew and secured as they successively made their appearance.

Resistance was of course offered by each, but in vain, for the thing was promptly and thoroughly carried out. Four strong men stood at the head of the companion with ropes ready to secure their prisoners, while the greater part of the crew stood close by armed with pistols and cutlasses.

"It is of no use resisting, Captain Blathers," said Griffin, when the former was pinioned; "you see we are quite prepared, and thoroughly in earnest."

The captain looked round, and a glance sufficed to convince him that this was true. Not a friendly eye met his, because those of the crew who were suspected of being favourable to him, or who could not be safely relied on, had been seized by another party of mutineers at the same time that those in the cabin were captured, and among them were three friends of our hero — Mr. Cupples the mate, Muggins, and Larry O'Hale, seamen belonging to the lost *Foam* to which Captain Dall had referred while conversing with Will.

For a few seconds Captain Blathers' face blazed with wrath, and he seemed about to make a desperate attempt to break his bonds, but by a strong effort he restrained himself.

"What do you intend to do?" he asked at length, in a deep, husky voice.

"To take possession of this ship," replied the second mate, with a slightly sarcastic smile. "These men have taken a fancy to lead a free, roving life, and to make me their captain, and I am inclined to fall in with their fancy, and to relieve you of the command."

"Scoundrel!" exclaimed the captain, "say rather that you have misled the men, and that —"

He checked himself, and then said sternly, "And pray what do you intend to do with *me*?"

"I shall allow you a boat and provisions, Captain Blathers, for the use of yourself and your friends, and then bid you farewell. You see we are mercifully inclined, and have no desire to shed your blood. Ho! there — lower one of the quarter boats."

This order was obeyed with promptitude. Some provisions were thrown into the boat, and the captain was cast loose and ordered to get into it. He turned to make a last appeal to the crew, but Griffin presented a pistol at his head and ordered him peremptorily to get into the boat. It is probable that he would have made another effort, had not two of the men forced him over the side. Seeing this, Will Osten was so indignant and so anxious to quit the ship, that he stepped forward with alacrity to follow him.

"No, no, my fine young fellow," said Griffin, thrusting him back, "we want your help as a doctor a little longer. It may be that you are not inclined to serve us, but we can find a way of compelling you if you're not. Come, Mr. Dall, be good enough to go next."

When Captain Dall's hands were loosed, he shook his fist in the second mate's face, and said, "Rascal, you'll swing for this yet; mark my words, you'll swing for it." Having relieved his feelings thus, he went over the side.

While this was going on, Larry O'Hale, Muggins, and Mr. Cupples, with several others, were brought to the gangway. Griffin addressed these before ordering them into the boat.

"My lads," he said, "I have no objection to your remaining aboard, if you choose to take part with us."

"I, for one, will have nothing to do with 'e," said Mr.

Cupples sternly.

"Then you may go," said Griffin, with a sneer. Muggins, who, to use one of his own phrases, looked "as sulky as a bear with a broken head," made no reply, but Larry O'Hale exclaimed, "Sure, then, what better can I do than take part with yees? It's a heavenly raigin o' the arth this, an good company. Put me down on the books, Capting Griffin, dear. I'd niver desart ye in your troubles, — be no mains."

There was a slight laugh at this, and Larry was graciously cast loose, and permitted to remain. Both Will Osten and Muggins gazed at him, however, in amazement, for they had supposed that their comrade would rather have taken his chance in the captain's boat. Suddenly an intelligent gleam shot athwart the rough visage of Muggins, and he said —

"Of coorse I'll remain too. It would be madness for an old salt like me to go paddlin' about the ocean in a cockleshell of a boat when he has the chance of sailin' in a good ship. Put me down too, capting. I'm game for anything a'most, from pitch an' toss to manslaughter."

So Muggins was added to the ship's company, and poor Mr. Cupples went over the side with a face almost as long as his thin body, because of what he deemed the depravity and desertion of his old shipmates. Several of the ship's crew, who refused to join, also went into the boat, which was then cast loose, and dropped rapidly astern.

The whole of this exciting scene passed so quickly, that it was only when the boat was far away, like a speck on the sea, that Will Osten realised the fact that he had actually said farewell, perhaps for over, to his late comrades. But he had not much time given him for reflection, for the new captain, after changing the course of the ship, and making a few arrangements to suit the altered state of affairs, ordered him to go forward and do duty as a common seaman, telling him that he did not intend to have any land-lubbers or idlers aboard, and that he would be called to do doctor's work when his services should be required.

That night our hero contrived to hold a whispering inter-view, in a dark corner of the forecastle, with his friends Larry O'Hale and Muggins. He found that the former had resolved to join the crew in order to be near himself; that Muggins had joined, because of his desire to share the fortunes of Larry; and that both had made up their minds to effect their escape on the first favourable opportunity.

"Now, ye see, boys," said Larry, "this is how it is —"

"Don't open your bread-basket hatch so wide," growled Muggins, "else you'll be overheerd — that's wot it is."

"This is how it is," repeated Larry, "not bein' fish, nor gulls, nor say sarpints, we haven't the ghost of a chance of gettin' away from this ship till we're close to land, an' even then we wont have much chance if it's suspected that we want to escape. What then? — why, let us from this hour agree to give each other the cowld shoulder, and go at our work as if we liked it."

"You're right, Larry," said Will. "If they see us much to-gether, they'll naturally suspect that we are plotting, so —"

At this point a voice growled from an adjacent hammock —

"Avast spinnin' yarns there, will 'e!"

"Ay, it's that sea-cook, Larry O'Hale," cried Muggins aloud; "he was always over fond o' talking."

Larry, who at the first sound had slipped away to his ham-mock, shouted from under the blankets, "Ye spalpeen, it's no more me than yersilf; sure I'd have been draimin' of ould Ireland if ye — hadn't — (snore) me grandmother — (yawn) or the pig —"

A prolonged snore terminated this sentence, and Muggins turned into his hammock, while Will Osten rose, with a quiet laugh, and went on deck.

One morning, some weeks after the conversation just related, our hero was leaning over the bulwarks near the fore-chains, watching the play of the clear waves as the ship glided quietly but swiftly through them before a light breeze. Will was in a meditative frame of mind, and had stood there gazing dreamily down for nearly half an hour, when his elbow was touched by the man named Bunco, who had long before recovered from his exposure in the canoe.

Will was a little surprised, for he had not had much intercourse with the man, and could not comprehend the confidential and peculiar look and tone with which he now addressed him.

"Mister Os'en," he said, in a low voice, after a few preliminary words, "you be tink of escape?"

Will was startled: "Why do you think so?" he asked, in some alarm.

"Ha!" said the man, with a broad grin, "me keep eyes in head — me doos — not in pocket. Ho! ho! Yis, me see an' hear berry well Muggins go too if hims can — and Larry O'Hale, ho yis. Now, me go too!"

"You too?"

"Yis. You save me life; me know dis here part ob the univarse, — bin bornded an' riz here. Not far off from de land to-day. You let me go too, an' me show you how you kin do —"

At this point Bunco was interrupted by a shout of "Land ho!" from the look-out at the masthead.

"Where away?" cried Griffin.

"On the lee-bow, sir."

Instantly all eyes and glasses were turned in the direction indicated, where, in a short time, a blue line, like a low cloud, was faintly seen on the far-off horizon.

CHAPTER III.

Describes a Tremendous but Bloodless Fight.

Proverbial philosophy tells us — and every one must have learned from personal experience — that "there is many a slip 'twixt the cup and the lip." Heroes in every rank of life are peculiarly liable to such slips, and *our* hero was no exception to the rule.

Finding that the vessel in which he sailed was now little, if at all, better than a pirate, he had fondly hoped that he should make his escape on the first point of South America at which they touched. Land was at last in sight. Hope was high in the breast of Will Osten, and expressive glances passed between him and his friends in captivity, when, alas! the land turned out to be a small island, so low that they could see right across it, and so scantily covered with vegetation that human beings evidently deemed it unworthy of being possessed.

"There's niver a sowl upon it," remarked Larry O'Hale, in a tone of chagrin.

"Maybe not," said Griffin, who overheard the observation; "but there's plenty of *bodies* on it if not souls, and, as we are short of provisions, I intend to lay-to, and give you a chance of seeing them. Get ready to go ashore; I'm not afraid of you *wandering too far!*"

Griffin wound up this speech with a low chuckle and a leer, which sent a chill to the heart not only of Will Osten but of Larry and Muggins also, for it convinced them that their new master had guessed their intention, and that he would, of course, take every precaution to prevent its being carried out. After the first depression of spirits, consequent on this discovery, the three friends became more than ever determined to outwit their enemy, and resolved to act, in the meantime, with perfect submission and prompt obedience — as they had hitherto done. Of course, each reserved in his own mind the right of rebellion if Griffin should require them to do any criminal act, and they hoped fervently that they should not fall in with any vessel that might prove a temptation to their new captain.

A few minutes after this, the order was given to lower one of the boats, and a crew jumped into her, among whom were Larry and Muggins. Will Osten asked permission to go, and Griffin granted his request with a grin that was the reverse of amiable.

"Musha! what sort o' bodies did the capting main?" said Larry, when they had pulled beyond earshot of the ship.

"Ha, paddy," replied one of the men, "they're pleasant fat bodies — amusin' to catch and much thought of by aldermen; — turtles no less."

"Ah! then, it's jokin' ye are."

"Not I. I never joke."

"Turthles is it — green fat an' all?"

"Ay, an' shells too."

"Sure it's for the coppers they're wanted."

"Just so, Larry, an' if you'll ship your oar an jump out wi' the painter, we'll haul the boat up an' show you how to catch 'em."

As the sailor spoke, the boat's keel grated on the sand, and the Irishman sprang over the side, followed by his comrades, who regarded the expedition in the light of a "good spree."

The party had to wait some time, however, for the anticipated sport. It was near sunset when they landed, but turtles are not always ready to deliver themselves up, even though the honour of being eaten by London aldermen sometimes awaits them! It is usually night before the creatures come out of the sea to enjoy a snooze on the beach. The men did not remain idle, however. They dragged the boat a considerable distance from the water, and then turned it keel up, supporting one gunwale on several forked sticks, so that a convenient shelter was provided. This look-out house was still further improved by having a soft carpet of leaves and grass spread beneath it.

When these preparations had been made, those men, who had never seen turtle-turning performed, were instructed in their duties by an experienced hand. The process being simple, the explanation was short and easy.

"You see, lads," said the instructor, leaning against the boat and stuffing down the glowing tobacco in his pipe with the point of his (apparently) fireproof little finger — "You see, lads, this is 'ow it is. All that you've got for to do is to keep parfitly still till the turtles comes out o' the sea, d'ye see? — then, as the Dook o' Wellin'ton said at Waterloo — Up boys an' at 'em! W'en, ov coorse, each man fixes his eyes on the turtle nearest him, runs out, ketches him by the rim of his shell an' turns him slap over on his back — d'ye understand?"

"Clear as ditch wather," said Larry.

"Humph!" said Muggins.

"Well, then, boys," continued the old salt with the fireproof little finger, "ye'd better go an' count the sand or the stars (when they comes out), for there won't be nothin' to do for an hour to come."

Having delivered himself thus, he refilled his pipe and lay down to enjoy it under the boat, while the others followed his example, or sauntered along the shore, or wandered among the bushes, until the time for action should arrive.

Will Osten and his two friends availed themselves of the opportunity to retire and hold an earnest consultation as to their future prospects and plans. As this was the first time they had enjoyed a chance of conversing without the fear of being over-heard, they made the most of it, and numerous were the projects which were proposed and rejected in eager earnest tones — at least on the part of Larry and Will. As for Muggins, although always earnest he was never eager. Tremendous indeed must have been the influence which could rouse him into a state of visible excite-ment! During the discussion the other two grew so warm that they forgot all about time and turtles, and would certainly have prolonged their talk for another hour had not one of the men appeared, telling them to clap a stopper on their potato-traps and return to the boat, as the sport was going to begin.

The moon had risen and commenced her course through a sky which was so clear that the planets shone like resplendent jewels, and the distant stars like diamond dust. Not a breath of air ruffled the surface of the sea; nevertheless, its slumbering ener-gies were indicated by the waves on the outlying coral reef, which, approaching one by one, slowly and solemnly, fell with what can only be called a quiet roar, hissed gently for a moment on the sand, and then passed with a sigh into absolute silence.

"Don't it seem as if the sea wor sleepin'," whispered one of the men, while they all lay watching under the boat.

"Ay, an' snorin' too," answered another.

"Whisht!" exclaimed a third, "if old Neptune hears ye, he'll wake up an' change his tune."

"Och, sure he's woke up already," whispered Larry, pointing with great excitement to a dark object which at that moment appeared to emerge from the sea.

"Mum's the word, boys," whispered the old salt who had charge of the party; "the critters are comin', an' England expec's every man for to do his dooty, as old Nelson said."

In the course of a few minutes several more dark objects emerged from the sea, and waddled with a kind of sigh or low grunt slowly up the beach, where they lay, evidently intending to have a nap! With breathless but eager interest, the sailors lay perfectly still, until fifteen of the dark objects were on the sands, and sufficient time was allowed them to fall into their first nap. Then the word "Turn" was given, and, leaping up, each man rushed swiftly but silently upon his prey! The turtles were pounced upon so suddenly that almost before they were wide awake they were caught; a bursting cheer followed, and instantly ten splendid animals were turned over on their backs, in which position, being unable to turn again, they lay flapping their flippers violently.

"That's the way to go it," shouted one of the men who, after turning his turtle, dashed after one of the other five which were now hastening back to the sea, with laborious but slow haste. His comrades followed suit instantly with a wild cheer. Now, to the uninitiated, this was the only moment of danger in that bloodless fight.

Being aware of his incapacity for swift flight, the turtle, when in the act of running away from danger, makes use of each flipper alternately in dashing the sand to an incredible height behind and around him, to the endangering of the pursuer's eyes, if he be not particularly careful. Sometimes incautious men have their eyes so filled with sand in this way that it almost blinds them for a time, and severe inflammation is occasionally the result.

The old salt — Peter Grant by name, but better known among his shipmates as Old Peter — was well aware of this habit of the turtle; but, having a spice of mischief in him, he said nothing about it. The consequences were severe on some of the men, particularly on Muggins. Our sedate friend was the only one who failed to turn a turtle at the first rush. He had tripped over a stone at starting, and when he gathered himself up and ran to the scene of action, the turtles were in full retreat. Burning with indignation at his bad fortune, he resolved to redeem his character; and, with this end in view, made a desperate rush at a particularly large turtle, which appeared almost too fat for its own shell. It chanced that Larry O'Hale, having already turned two, also set his affections on this turtle, and made a rush at it; seeing which Muggins slyly ran behind him, tripped up his heels, and passed on.

"Have a care," cried Will Osten, laughing, "he'll bite!"

"Bad luck to yez!" shouted Larry, leaping up, and following hard on Muggins' heels.

Just then the turtle began to use his flippers in desperation. Sand flew in all directions. The pursuers, nothing daunted though surprised, partially closed their eyes, bent down their heads, and advanced. Larry opened his mouth to shout — a shower of sand filled it. He opened his eyes in astonishment — another shower shut them both up, causing him to howl while he coughed and spluttered. But Muggins pressed on valorously.

One often reads, in the history of war, of brave and reckless heroes who go through "storms of shot and shell" almost scathless, while others are falling like autumn leaves around them. Something similar happened on the present occasion. While Larry and several of the other men were left behind, pitifully and tenderly picking the sand out of their eyes, the bold Muggins — covered with sand from head to foot, but still not mortally wounded — advanced singlehanded against the foe — rushed at the turtle; tripped over it; rose again; quailed for a second before the tremendous fire; burst through it, and, finally, catching the big creature by the rim, turned him on his back, and uttered a roar rather than a cheer of triumph.

This was the last capture made that night. Immediately after their victory the men returned to the boat, where they kindled an immense bonfire and prepared to spend the night, leaving the turtles to kick helplessly on their backs till the morning light should enable them to load the boat and return with their prizes to the ship. Meanwhile pipes were loaded and lit, and Doctor Will, as Old Peter called him, looked after the wounded.

CHAPTER IV.

In which Another Fight is recorded and an Escape is made, but whether Fortunate or the Reverse Remains to be seen.

The supply of fresh meat thus secured was very acceptable to the crew of the *Rover*, and their circumstances were further improved by the addition of a number of fresh cocoa-nuts which were collected on the island by Bunco, that individual being the only one on board who could perform, with ease, the difficult feat of climbing the cocoa-nut palms. After a couple of days spent at this island, the *Rover* weighed anchor and stood away for the coast of South America, which she sighted about two weeks afterwards.

Here, one evening, they were becalmed not far from land, and Griffin ordered a boat to be lowered, with a crew to go ashore. The captain had been in low spirits that day, from what cause was not known, and no one ever found out the reason, but certain it is that he was unusually morose and gruff. He was also rather absent, and did not observe the fact that Larry O'Hale, Muggins, and Will Osten were among the crew of the boat. The mate observed it, however, and having a shrewd suspicion of their intentions, ordered them to leave it.

"What said you?" asked Griffin of the mate, as he was about to go over the side.

"I was about to change some of the crew," he replied confidentially. "It would be as well to keep O'Hale and —"

"Oh, never mind," said Griffin roughly, "let 'em go."

The mate, of course, stepped back, and Griffin got into the boat, which was soon on its way to the land. On nearing the shore, it was found that a tremendous surf broke upon the beach — owing to its exposure to the long rolling swell of the Pacific. When the boat, which was a small one, entered this surf, it became apparent that the attempt to land was full of danger. Each wave that bore them on its crest for a second and then left them behind was so gigantic that nothing but careful steering could save them from turning broadside on and being rolled over like a cask. Griffin was a skilful steersman, but he evidently was not at that time equal to the occasion. He steered wildly. When they were close to the beach the boat upset. Every man swam towards a place where a small point of land caused a sort of eddy and checked the force of the undertow. They all reached it in a few minutes, with the exception of Griffin, who had found bottom on a sand-bank, and stood, waist deep, laughing, apparently, at the struggles of his comrades.

"You'd better come ashore," shouted one of the men.

Griffin replied by another laugh, in the midst of which he sank suddenly and disappeared. It might have been a quicksand — it might have been a shark — no one ever could tell, but the unhappy man had gone to his account — he was never more seen!

The accident had been observed from the ship, and the mate at once lowered a boat and hastened to the rescue. Those on shore observed this, and awaited its approach. Before it was half way from the beach, however, Peter Grant said to his comrades —

"I'll tell 'e wot it is, boys; seems to me that Providence has given us a chance of gittin' away from that ship. I never was a pirate, an' I don't mean for to become one, so, all who are of my way of thinkin' come over here."

Will Osten and his friends were so glad to find that a shipmate had, unknown to them, harboured thoughts of escaping, that they at once leaped to his side, but none of the others followed. They were all determined, reckless men, and had no intention of giving up their wild course. Moreover, they were not prepared to allow their comrades to go off quietly. One of them, in particular, a very savage by nature, as well as a giant, stoutly declared that he not only meant to stick by the ship himself, but would compel the others to do so too, and for this purpose placed himself between them and the woods, which, at that part of the coast, approached close to the sea. Those who took his part joined him, and for a few moments the two parties stood gazing at each other in silence. There was good ground for hesitation on both sides, for, on the one hand, Will Osten and his three friends were resolute and powerful fellows, while, on the other, the giant and his comrades, besides being stout men, were eight in number. Now, it chanced that our hero had, in early boyhood, learned an art which, we humbly submit, has been unfairly brought into disrepute — we refer to the art of boxing. Good reader, allow us to state that we do not advocate pugilism. We never saw a prize-fight, and have an utter abhorrence of the "ring." We not only dislike the idea of seeing two men pommel each other's faces into a jelly, but we think the looking at such a sight tends to demoralise. There is a vast difference, however, between this and the use of "the gloves," by means of which a man may learn the useful art of "self-defence," and may, perhaps, in the course of his life, have the happiness of applying his knowledge to the defence of a mother, a sister, or a wife, as well as "self." If it be objectionable to use the gloves because they represent the fist, then is it equally objectionable to use the foil because it represents the sword? But, pray, forgive this digression. Ten to one, in *your* case, reader, it is unnecessary, because sensible people are more numerous than foolish! Howbeit, whether right or wrong, Will Osten had, as we have said, acquired the by no means unimportant knowledge of *where* to hit and *how* to hit. He had also the good sense to discern *when* to hit, and he invariably acted on the principal that — "whatever is worth doing, is worth doing well."

On the present occasion Will walked suddenly up to the giant, and, without uttering a word, planted upon his body two blows, which are, we believe, briefly termed by the "fancy" *one — two*! We do not pretend to much knowledge on this point, but we are quite certain that number *one* lit upon the giant's chest and took away his breath, while number *two* fell upon his forehead and removed his senses. Before he had time to recover either breath or senses, number *three* ended the affair by flattening his nose and stretching his body on the sand.

At this sudden and quite unexpected proceeding Larry O'Hale burst into a mingled laugh and cheer, which he appropriately concluded by springing on and flooring the man who stood opposite to him. Muggins and the old salt were about to follow his example, but their opponents turned and fled, doubling on their tracks and making for the boat. Larry, Muggins, and Old Peter, being thoroughly roused, would have followed them regardless of consequences, and undoubtedly would have been overpowered by numbers (for the boat had just reached the shore), had not Will Osten bounded ahead of them, and, turning round, shouted energetically —

"Follow me, lads, if you would be free. Now or never!"

Luckily the tone in which Will said this impressed them so much that they stopped in their wild career; and when they looked back and saw their young friend running away towards the woods as fast as his legs could carry him, and heard the shout of the reinforced seamen as they started from the water's edge to give chase, they hesitated no longer. Turning round, they also fled. It is, however, due to Larry O'Hale to say that he shook his fist at the enemy, and uttered a complex howl of defiance before turning tail!

Well was it for all of them that day that the woods were near, and that they were dense and intricate. Old Peter, although a sturdy man, and active for his years, was not accustomed to running, and had no wind for a race with young men.

His comrades would never have deserted him, so that all would have certainly been captured but for a fortunate accident. They had not run more than half a mile, and their pursuers were gaining on them at every stride — as they could tell by the sound of their voices — when Will Osten, who led, fell headlong into a deep hole that had been concealed by rank undergrowth. Old Peter, who was close at his heels, fell after him, and Larry, who followed Peter to encourage and spur him on, also tumbled in. Muggins alone was able to stop short in time.

"Hallo, boys!" he cried in a hoarse whisper, "are yer timbers damaged?"

"Broke to smithereens," groaned Larry from the abyss.

Will Osten, who had scrambled out in a moment, cried hastily, "Jump in, Muggins. I'll lead 'em off the scent. Stop till I return, boys, d'ye hear?"

"Ay, ay," said Larry.

Away went Will at right angles to their former course, uttering a shout of defiance, only just in time, for the mate of the *Rover*, who led the chase, was close on him. Soon the sounds told those in hiding that the *ruse* had been successful. The sounds died away in the distance and the deep silence of the forest succeeded — broken only now and then by the cry of some wild animal.

Meanwhile, our hero used his legs so well that he not only left his pursuers out of sight and hearing behind, but circled gradually around until he returned to the hole where his comrades lay. Here they all remained for nearly an hour, and then, deeming themselves safe, issued forth none the worse of their tumble. They commenced to return to the coast, having settled that this was their wisest course, and that they could easily avoid their late comrades by keeping well to the northward. This devia-tion, however, was unfortunate. Those who have tried it know well how difficult it is to find one's way in a dense forest. The more they attempted to get out of the wood the deeper they got into it, and at length, when night began to close in, they were forced to come to the conclusion that they were utterly lost — lost in the forest — "a livin' example," as Larry O'Hale expressed it, "of the babes in the wood!"

CHAPTER V.

Shows what the Lost Ones did,
and how they were Found.

The condition of being "lost" is a sad one in any circumstances, but being lost in a forest — a virgin forest — a forest of unknown extent, in a vast continent such as that of South America, must be admitted to be a peculiarly severe misfortune. Nevertheless, we are bound to say that our hero and his friends did not appear to regard their lost condition in this light. Perhaps their indifference arose partly from their ignorance of what was entailed in being lost in the forest. The proverb says, that "where ignorance is bliss 'tis folly to be wise." Whether that be true or not, there can be no question that it is sometimes an advantage to be ignorant. Had our lost friends known the extent of the forest in which they were lost, the number of its wild four-footed inhabitants, and the difficulties and dangers that lay before them, it is certain that they could not have walked along as light-heartedly as they did, and it is probable that they would have been less able to meet those difficulties and dangers when they appeared.

Be this as it may, Will Osten and Larry O'Hale, Muggins, and Old Peter, continued to wander through the forest, after discovering that they were lost, until the increasing darkness rendered further progress impossible; then they stopped and sat down on the stump of a fallen tree.

"It is clear," said our hero, "that we shall have to pass the night here, for there is no sign of human habitation, and the light is failing fast."

"That's so," said Muggins curtly.

"I'm a'feard on it," observed Old Peter with a sigh.

"Faix, I wouldn't mind spindin' the night," said Larry, "av it worn't that we've got no grub. It would be some comfort to know the name o' the country we're lost in."

"I can tell you that, Larry," said Will Osten; "we are in Peru; though what part of it I confess I do not know."

"Peroo, is it? Well, that's a comfort — anyhow."

"I don't 'xacly see where the comfort o' that lies," said Muggins.

"That's cause yer intellects is obtoose, boy!" retorted Larry; "don't ye know that it's a blissin' to know where ye are, wotiver else ye don't know? Supposin', now, a stranger shud ax me, 'Where are ye, Paddy?' — ov course I cud say at wance, 'In Peroo, yer honour;' an' if he shud go for to penetrate deeper into my knowledge o' geography, sure I cud tell him that Peroo is in South Ameriky, wan o' the five quarters o' the globe, d'ye see?"

"But suppose, for the sake of argyment as Shikspur says, that the stranger wos to ax ye wot ye know'd about Peroo, what 'ud ye say to that, lad?" asked Old Peter.

"Wot would I say! Why, I'd ax him with a look of offended dignity if he took me for a schoolmaster, an' then may be I'd ax him wot he know'd about it himself — an' krekt him av he wos wrong."

"I can tell you this much about it, at all events," said Will, with a laugh, "that it is a Republic, and a celebrated country for gold mines."

"And I can add to yer information," said Old Peter, "that there's an oncommon lot o' tigers an' other wild beasts in it, and that if we would avoid bein' eat up alive we must kindle a fire an' go to sleep in a tree. By good luck I've got my flint and steel with me."

"By equal good luck I have two biscuits in my pocket," said Will; "come, before we do anything else, let us inquire into our resources."

Each man at once turned his pockets inside out with the following result: —

Our hero, besides two large coarse sea-biscuits, produced one of those useful knives which contain innumerable blades, with pickers, tweezers, corkscrews, and other indescribable implements; also a note-book, a pencil, a small pocket-case of surgical instruments (without which he never moved during his wanderings), and a Testament — the one that had been given to him on his last birthday by his mother. Old Peter contributed to the general fund his flint, steel, and tinder — most essential and fortunate contributions — and a huge clasp-knife. Indeed we may omit the mention of knives in this record, for each man possessed one as a matter of course. It was by no means a matter of course, however, but a subject of intense gratification to at least three of the party, that Muggins had two pipes and an unusually large supply of tobacco. Larry also had a short black pipe and a picker, besides a crooked sixpence, which he always kept about him "for luck," a long piece of stout twine, and a lump of cheese. The sum total was not great, but was extremely useful in the circumstances.

All this wealth having been collected together, it was agreed that the biscuits, cheese, tobacco, and pipes should be common property. They were accordingly divided with the utmost care by Will, who, by the way, did not require a pipe as he was not a smoker. We do not record this as an evidence of his superior purity! By no means. Will Osten, we regret to say, was not a man of strong principle. All the principle he had, and the good feelings which actuated him, were the result of his mother's teaching — not of his own seeking. He did not smoke because his had discouraged smoking, therefore — not having acquired the habit — he disliked it. Thousands of men might (and would) have been free from this habit to-day had they been affectionately dissuaded from it in early youth. So, too, in reference to his Testament — Will always carried it about with him, not because he valued it much for its own sake, or read it often, but because it was the last gift he received from his mother. It reminded him of her; besides, it was small and did not take up much room in his pocket. Blessed influence of mothers! If they only knew the greatness of their power, and were more impressed with the importance of using it for the glory of God, this would be a happier world!

The costume of these wanderers, like their small possessions, was varied. All wore white duck trousers and blue Guernsey or cotton shirts with sou'-westers or straw hats, but the coats and cravats differed. Larry wore a rough pilot-cloth coat, and, being eccentric on the point, a scarlet cotton neckerchief. Old Peter wore a blue jacket with a black tie, loosely fastened, sailor fashion, round his exposed throat. Muggins wore the dirty canvas jacket in which he had been engaged in scraping down the masts of the *Rover* when he left her. Will Osten happened to have on a dark blue cloth shooting-coat and a white straw hat, which was fortunate, for, being in reality the leader of the party, it was well that his costume should accord with that responsible and dignified position. They had no weapons of any kind, so their first care was to supply themselves with stout cudgels, which each cut in proportion to his notions of the uses and capacities of such implements — that of Larry O'Hale being, of course, a genuine shillelah, while the weapon cut by Muggins was a close imitation of the club of Hercules, or of that used by the giant who was acquainted with the celebrated giant-killer named Jack!

"Now, boys, if we're goin' to ait and slaip, the sooner we set about it the better," observed Larry, rising and commencing to collect sticks for a fire. The others immediately followed his example, and in a few minutes a bright blaze illuminated the dark recesses of the tangled forest, while myriads of sparks rose into and hung upon the leafy canopy overhead. There was something cheering as well as romantic in this. It caused the wanderers to continue their work with redoubled vigour. Soon a fire that would have roasted an ox whole roared and sent its forked tongues upwards. In the warm blaze of it they sat down to their uncommonly meagre supper of half a biscuit and a small bit of cheese each — which was washed down by a draught from a neighbouring stream.

They had finished this, and were in the act of lighting their pipes, when a roar echoed through the woods which caused them to pause in their operations and glance uneasily at each other.

"Sure, it's a tiger!" exclaimed Larry.

"There's no tigers in them parts," said Muggins.

"I don't know that, lad," observed Old Peter.

"I've hear'd that there are jaguars an' critters o' that sort, which is as big and as bad as tigers, an' goes by the name, but p'raps —"

Old Peter's observations were here cut short by the loud report of a gun close at hand. As if by instinct every man leaped away from the light of the fire and sheltered himself behind a tree. For some time they stood listening eagerly to every sound, but no foe appeared, nor was there a repetition of the shot. The longer they listened the more inclined were they to believe that their senses had deceived them, and Larry O'Hale's heart was beginning to make a troublesome attack on his ribs, as he thought of ghosts — especially foreign ghosts — when all eyes were attracted to a human form which appeared to flit to and fro among the tree stems in the distance, as if to avoid the strong light of the fire.

Knowing that one man with a gun could make certain of shooting the whole party if he chose, and that he would not be more likely to attempt violence if trust in his generosity were displayed, Will Osten, with characteristic impetuosity, suddenly walked into the full blaze of the firelight and made signals to the stranger to approach. Larry and the others, although they disapproved of the rashness of their young leader, were not the men to let him face danger alone. They at once joined him, and awaited the approach of the apparition.

It advanced slowly, taking advantage of every bush and tree, and keeping its piece always pointed towards the fire. They observed that it was black and partially naked.

Suddenly Muggins exclaimed — "I do b'lieve it's —" He paused.

"Sure, it's the nigger — och! av it isn't Bunco!" cried Larry.

Bunco it was, sure enough, and the moment he perceived that he was recognised, he discarded all precaution, walked boldly into the encampment, and shook them all heartily by the hand.

CHAPTER VI.

Bunco becomes a Friend in Need and indeed,
and Larry "comes to Grief" in a Small Way.

"Sure yer face is a sight for sore eyes, though it *is* black and ugly," exclaimed Larry, as he wrung the hand of the good-humoured native, who grinned from ear to ear with delight at having found his friends.

"Wot ever brought ye here?" inquired Muggins.

"Mine legses," replied Bunco, with a twinkle in his coal-black eyes.

"Yer legses, eh?" repeated Muggins in a tone of sarcasm — "so I supposes, for it's on them that a man usually goeses; but what caused you for to desart the ship?"

"'Cause I no want for be pyrit more nor yourself, Mister Muggles —"

"Muggins, you lump of ebony — don't miscall me."

"Well, dat be all same — only a litil bit more ogly," retorted Bunco, with a grin, "an' me no want to lose sight ob Doctor Os'n here: me come for to show him how to go troo de forest."

"That's right, my good fellow," cried Will, with a laugh, slapping the native on the shoulder; "you have just come in the nick of time to take care of us all, for, besides having utterly lost ourselves, we are quite ignorant of forest ways in this region — no better than children, in fact."

"True for ye, boy, riglar babes in the wood, as I said before," added Larry O'Hale.

"Well, that being the case," continued Will, "you had better take command at once, Bunco, and show us how to encamp, for we have finished our pipes and a very light supper, and would fain go to sleep. It's a pity you did not arrive sooner, my poor fellow, for we have not a scrap of food left for you, and your gun will be of no use till daylight."

To this Bunco replied by displaying his teeth and giving vent to a low chuckle, while he lifted the flap of his pea-jacket and exhibited three fat birds hanging at the belt with which he supported his nether garments.

"Hooray!" shouted Larry, seizing one of the birds and beginning to pluck it; "good luck to your black mug, we'll ait it right off."

"That's your sort," cried Muggins, whose mouth watered at the thought of such a delightful addition to his poor supper. "Hand me one of 'em, Larry, and I'll pluck it."

Larry obeyed; Old Peter seized and operated on the last bird, and Bunco raked the embers of the fire together, while Will Osten looked on and laughed. In a very few minutes the three birds were plucked and cleaned, and Larry, in virtue of his office, was going to cook them, when Will suggested that he had better resign in favour of Bunco, who was doubtless better acquainted than himself with the best modes of forest cookery. To this Larry objected a little at first, but he was finally prevailed on to give in, and Bunco went to work in his own fashion. It was simple enough. First he cut three short sticks and pointed them at each end, then he split each bird open, and laying it flat, thrust a stick through it, and stuck it up before the glowing fire to roast. When one side was pretty well done he turned the other, and, while that was cooking, cut off a few scraps from the half-roasted side and tried them.

We need scarcely add that none of the party were particular.

The birds were disposed of in an incredibly short time, and then the pipes were refilled for a second smoke.

"How comes it," inquired Will, when this process was going on, "that you managed to escape and to bring a gun away with you? We would not have left the ship without you, but our own escape was a sudden affair; we scarcely expected to accomplish it at the time we did. I suppose you had a sharp run for it?"

"Run! ductor, no, me no run — me walk away quite comfrabil an' tooked what me please; see here."

As he spoke, Bunco opened a small canvas bag which no one had taken notice of up to that moment, and took from it a large quantity of broken biscuit, a lump of salt beef, several cocoa-nuts, a horn of gunpowder, and a bag of shot and ball — all of which he spread out in front of the fire with much ostentation. The satisfaction caused by this was very great, and even Muggins, in the fulness of his heart, declared that after all there were worse things than being lost in a forest.

"Well, and how did you manage to get away?" said Will, returning to the original question.

"Git away? why, dis here wos de way. When me did see the rincumcoshindy goin' on ashore, me say, 'Now, Bunco, you time come; look alive;' so, w'en de raskil called de fuss mate orders out de boat in great hurry, me slip into it like one fish. Then dey all land an' go off like mad into de woods arter you — as you do knows. Ob coorse me stop to look arter de boat; you knows it would be very bad to go an' leave de boat all by its lone, so w'en deys gone into de woods, me take the mate's gun and poodair an' shot an' ebbery ting could carry off — all de grub, too, but der worn't too moche of dat — and walk away in anoder d'rection. Me is used to de woods, you sees, so kep' clear o' de stoopid seamans, who soon tires der legses, as me knows bery well; den come round in dis d'rection; find you tracks; foller im up; shoots tree birds; sees a tiger; puts a ball in him skin, an' sends him to bed wid a sore head — too dark for kill him — arter which me find you out, an' here me is. Dere. Dat's all about it."

"A most satisfactory account of yourself," said Will Osten.

"An' purtily towld," observed Larry; "where did ye larn English, boy, for ye have the brogue parfict, as me gran'mother used to say to the pig when she got in her dotage (me gran'mother, not the pig), 'only,' says she, 'the words isn't quite distinc'.' Couldn't ye give us a skitch o' yer life, Bunco?"

Thus appealed to, the gratified native began without hesitation, and gave the following account of himself:

"Me dun know when me was born —"

"Faix, it wasn't yesterday," said Larry, interrupting.

"No, nor de day before to-morrow nother," retorted Bunco; "but it was in Callyforny, anyhow. Me fadder him wos a Injin —"

"Oh! come!" interrupted Muggins in a remonstrative tone.

"Yis, him *wos* a Injin," repeated Bunco stoutly.

"Wos he a *steam-ingine?*" inquired Muggins with a slight touch of sarcasm.

"He means an Indian, Muggins," explained Will.

"Then why don't he say wot he means? However, go ahead, Ebony."

"Hims wos a Injin," resumed Bunco, "ant me moder him wos a Spanish half-breed from dis yer country — Peru. Me live for years in de forests an' plains an' mountains ob Callyforny huntin' an fightin'. Oh, dem were de happy days! After dat me find a wife what I lub berry moche, den me leave her for short time an' go wid tradin' party to de coast. Here meet wid a cap'n of ship, wot wos a big raskil. Him 'tice me aboord an' sail away. Short ob hands him wos, so him took me, an' me never see me wife no more!"

There was something quite touching in the tone in which

the poor fellow said this, insomuch that Larry became sympathetic and abused the captain who had kidnapped him in no measured terms. Had Larry known that acts similar to this wicked and heartless one were perpetrated by traders in the South Seas very frequently, he would have made his terms of abuse more general!

"How long ago was that?" inquired Old Peter.

"Tree year," sighed Bunco. "Since dat day I hab bin in two tree ships, but nebber run away, cause why? wot's de use ob run away on *island*? Only now me got on Sout 'Meriky, which me know is not far from Nord 'Meriky, an' me bin here before wid me moder, so kin show you how to go — and speak Spanish too — me moder speak dat, you sees; but mesilf larn English aboord two tree ships, an', so, speak him fust rate now."

"So ye do, boy," said Larry, whose sympathetic heart was drawn towards the unfortunate and ill-used native; "an', faix, we'll go on travellin' through this forest till we comes to Cally-forny an' finds your missus — so cheer up, Bunco, and let us see how we're to go to roost, for it seems that we must slaip on a tree this night."

During the course of the conversation which we have just detailed, the wild denizens of the forest had been increasing their dismal cries, and the seamen, unused to such sounds, had been kept in a state of nervous anxiety which each did his utmost to conceal. They were all brave men; but it requires a very peculiar kind of bravery to enable a man to sit and listen with cool indifference to sounds which he does not understand, issuing from gloomy recesses at his back, where there are acknowledged, though unknown, dangers close at hand. Bunco, therefore, grinning good-humouredly as usual, rose and selected a gigantic tree as their dormitory.

The trunk of this tree spread out, a few feet above its base, into several branches, any one of which would have been deemed a large tree in England, and these branches were again subdivided into smaller stems with a network of foliage, which rendered it quite possible for a man to move about upon them with facility, and to find a convenient couch. Here, — the fire at the foot of the tree having been replenished, — each man sought and found repose.

It was observed that Larry O'Hale made a large soft couch below the tree on the ground.

"You're not going to sleep there, Larry?" said Will Osten, on observing what he was about. "Why, the tigers will be picking your bones before morning if you do."

"Och! I'm not afraid of 'em," replied Larry; "howsever, I *do* main to slaip up the tree *if I can.*"

That night, some time after all the party had been buried in profound repose, they were awakened by a crash and a tremendous howl just below them. Each started up, and, pushing aside the leaves, gazed anxiously down. A dark object was seen moving below, and Bunco was just going to point his gun at it, when a gruff voice was heard to say —

"Arrah! didn't I know it? It's famous I've bin, since I was a mere boy, for rowlin' about in me slaip, an', sure, the branch of a tree is only fit for a bird after all. But, good luck to yer wisdom an' foresight, Larry O'Hale, for ye've come down soft, anyhow, an' if there's anything'll cure ye o' this bad habit — slaipin' on trees'll do it in the coorse o' time, I make no doubt wotiver!"

CHAPTER VII.

Wherein are recounted Dangers, Difficulties, and Perplexities faced and Overcome.

Next morning the travellers rose with the sun and descended from the tree in which they had spent the night — much refreshed and "ready for anything."

It was well that they were thus prepared for whatever might befall them, for there were several incidents in store for them that day which tried them somewhat, and would have perplexed them sadly had they been without a guide. Perhaps we are scarcely entitled to bestow that title on Bunco, for he was as thoroughly lost in the forest as were any of his companions, in the sense, at least, of being ignorant as to where he was, or how far from the nearest human habitation: but he was acquainted with forest-life, knew the signs and symptoms of the wilderness, and could track his way through pathless wastes in a manner that was utterly incomprehensible to his companions, and could not be explained by himself. Moreover, he was a shrewd fellow, as well as bold, and possessed a strong sense of humour, which he did not fail at times to gratify at the expense of his friends.

This tendency was exhibited by him in the first morning's march, during which he proved his superiority in woodcraft, and firmly established himself in the confidence of the party. The incident occurred thus:

After a hearty and hasty breakfast — for, being lost, they were all anxious to get found as soon as possible — they set forth in single file; Bunco leading, Old Peter, Muggins, and Larry following, and Will Osten bringing up the rear. During the first hour they walked easily and pleasantly enough through level and rather open woodland, where they met few obstacles worth mentioning, so that Larry and Muggins, whose minds were filled with the idea of wild beasts, and who were much excited by the romance of their novel position, kept a sharp lookout on the bushes right and left, the one shouldering his gigantic cudgel, the other flourishing his shillelah in a humorous free-and-easy way, and both feeling convinced that with such weapons they were more than a match for any tiger alive! When several hours had elapsed, however, without producing any sign or sound of game, they began to feel disappointment, and to regard their guide as an exaggerator if not worse; and when, in course of time, the underwood became more dense and their passage through the forest more difficult, they began to make slighting remarks about their dark-skinned friend, and to question his fitness for the duties of guide. In particular, Muggins — who was becoming fatigued, owing partly to the weight of his club as well as to the weight of his body and the shortness of his legs — at last broke out on him and declared that he would follow no further.

"Why," said he gruffly, "it's as plain as the nose on yer nutmeg face, that ye're steerin' a wrong coorse. You'll never make the coast on this tack."

"Oh yis, wees will," replied Bunco, with a quiet smile.

"No, wees won't, ye lump o' mahogany," retorted Muggins. "Don't the coast run nor' and by west here away?"

"Troo," assented Bunco with a nod.

"Well, and ain't we goin' due north just now, so that the coast lies away on our left, an' for the last three hours you've bin bearin' away to the *right*, something like nor' and by east, if it's not nor' *east* an' by east, the coast being all the while on yer port beam, you grampus — that's so, ain't it?"

"Yis, dat's so," replied Bunco with a grin.

"Then, shiver my timbers, why don't ye shove yer helm hard a starboard an' lay yer right coorse? Come, lads, *I'll* go to the wheel now for a spell."

Will Osten was about to object to this, but Bunco gave him a peculiar glance which induced him to agree to the proposal; so Muggins went ahead and the rest followed.

At the place where this dispute occurred there chanced to be a stretch of comparatively open ground leading away to the left. Into this glade the hardy seamen turned with an air of triumph.

His triumph, however, was short-lived, for at a turn in the glade he came to a place where the underwood was so dense and so interlaced with vines and creeping plants that further advance was absolutely impossible. After "yawing about" for some minutes "in search of a channel," as Larry expressed it, Muggins suddenly gave in and exclaimed, — "I'm a Dutchman, boys, if we ha'n't got embayed!"

"It's let go the anchor an' take soundin's 'll be the nixt order, I s'pose, Captain Muggins?" said Larry, touching his cap.

"Or let the tother pilot take the helm," said Old Peter, "'he's all my fancy painted him,' as Milton says in Paraphrases Lost."

"Right, Peter," cried Will Osten, "we must dethrone Muggins and reinstate Bunco."

"Ha! you's willin' for to do second fiddil *now*?" said the native, turning with a grin to Muggins, as he was about to resume his place at the head of the party.

"No, never, ye leather-jawed kangaroo, but I've no objections to *do* the drum on yer skull, with *this* for a drumstick!" He flourished his club as he spoke, and Bunco, bounding away with a laugh, led the party back on their track for a few paces, then, turning sharp to the right, he conducted them into a narrow opening in the thicket, and proceeded in a zig-zag manner that utterly confused poor Muggins, inducing him from that hour to resign himself with blind faith to the guidance of his conqueror. Well would it be for humanity in general, and for rulers in particular, if there were more of Muggins's spirit abroad inducing men to give in and resign cheerfully when beaten fairly!

If the sailors were disappointed at not meeting with any wild creatures during the first part of their walk, they were more than compensated by the experiences of the afternoon. While they were walking quietly along, several snakes — some of considerable length — wriggled out of their path, and Larry trod on one which twirled round his foot, causing him to leap off the ground like a grasshopper and utter a yell, compared to which all his previous shoutings were like soft music. Bunco calmed his fears, however, and comforted the party by saying that these snakes were harmless. Nevertheless, they felt a strong sensation of aversion to the reptiles, which it was not easy to overcome, and Muggins began to think seriously that being lost in the forest was, after all, a pleasure mingled considerably with alloy! Not long after the incident of the snake, strange sounds were heard from time to time in the bushes, and all the party, except Bunco, began to glance uneasily from side to side, and grasped their weapons firmly. Suddenly a frightful-looking face was observed by Larry peeping through the bushes right over Muggins's unconscious head. The horrified Irishman, who thought it was no other than a visitant from the world of fiends, was going to utter a shout of warning, when a long hairy arm was stretched out from the bushes and Muggins's hat was snatched from his head.

"Och! ye spalpeen," cried Larry, hurling his cudgel at the ugly creature.

The weapon was truly aimed; it hit the monkey on the back, causing it to drop the hat and vanish from the spot — shrieking.

"Well done, Larry!" cried Will Osten; "why didn't you warn us to expect visits from such brutes, Bunco?"

"Why, cause me tink you know all 'bout 'im. Hab larn 'im from Jo Gruffy."

"From who?"

"From Jo Gruffy. Him as you was say, last night, do tell all 'bout de countries ob de world, and wot sort of treeses an' hanimals in 'im. Der be plenty ob dem hanimals — (how you call 'im, mongkees?) in Peroo, big an leetil."

"Well!" exclaimed our hero with a laugh, "possibly geography may refer to the fact; if so, I had forgotten it, but I'm sorry to hear that they are numerous, for they are much too bold to be pleasant companions."

"Dey do us no harm," said Bunco, grinning, "only chok full ob fun!"

"Git along wid ye," cried Larry. "It's my belaif they're yer own relations, or ye wouldn't stick up for them."

Thus admonished, the native resumed the march, and led them through the jungle into deeper and darker shades. Here the forest was quite free from underwood, and the leafy canopy overhead was so dense that the sky could seldom be seen. Everything appeared to be steeped in a soft mellow shade of yellowish green, which was delightfully cool and refreshing in a land lying so very near to the equator. The howling and hoarse barking of wild beasts was now heard to an extent that fully satisfied Larry O'Hale and his friend Muggins. There were patches of dense jungle here and there, in which it was supposed the animals lay concealed, and each of these were carefully examined by our travellers. That there was need for caution became apparent from the fact that Bunco carried his gun at full cock in the hollow of his left arm, and had a stern, earnest expression of visage which was quite new to his nautical companions, and made a deep impres-

sion on them. Curious and interesting change of sentiment —
the man whom, while at sea, they had treated with good-
humoured contempt, was ere long clung to and regarded almost
with reverence!

"Be quiet, boys, here," he said, "an' no make noise. Keep de
eyes open."

After this he did not speak, but gave his directions by signs.

CHAPTER VIII.

In which Bunco displays Uncommon Valour, and Tigers come to Grief.

Advancing cautiously, the travellers arrived at the brink of a dark ravine, in the bottom of which there was a good deal of brushwood, with here and there several pools of water. They had remained a short time here on the top of the bank, listening to the various barks and cries of the wild animals around them, when their attention was arrested by several loud yelps, which sounded as if some creature were approaching them fast. Bunco signed to them to stoop and follow him. They did so, and had not advanced a hundred yards when the loud clatter of hoofs was heard. Bunco crouched instantly and held his gun in readiness, while his black eyes glittered and his expressive features seemed to blaze with eagerness. His followers also crouched among the bushes, and each grasped his club with a feeling that it was but a poor weapon of defence after all — though better than nothing!

They had not to wait long, for, in a few minutes, a beautiful black wild horse came racing like the wind along the clear part of the ravine in the direction of the place where they were concealed. The magnificent creature was going at his utmost speed, being pursued by a large tiger, and the steam burst from his distended nostrils, while his voluminous mane and tail waved wildly in the air. The tiger gained on him rapidly. Its bounds were tremendous; at each leap it rose several feet from the ground. The poor horse was all but exhausted, for he slipped and came down on his knees, when abreast of, and not thirty yards distant from, the place where the travellers lay. The tiger did not miss his opportunity. He crouched and ran along with the twisting motion of a huge cat; then he sprang a clear distance of twenty feet and alighted on the horse's back, seizing him by the neck with a fearful growl. Now came Bunco's opportunity. While the noble horse reared and plunged violently in a vain attempt to get rid of his enemy, the cautious native took a steady aim, and was so long about it that some of the party nearly lost patience with him. At last he fired, and the tiger fell off the horse, rolling and kicking about in all directions — evidently badly wounded. The horse meanwhile galloped away and was soon lost to view.

Instead of loading and firing again, Bunco threw down his gun, and, drawing a long knife, rushed in upon his victim. His comrades, who thought him mad, sprang after him, but he had closed with the tiger and plunged his knife into it before they came up. The creature uttered a tremendous roar and writhed rapidly about, throwing up clouds of dust from the dry ground, while Bunco made another dash at him and a plunge with his long knife, but he missed the blow and fell. His comrades closed in and brandished their clubs, but the rapid motions of man and beast rendered it impossible for them to strike an effective blow without running the risk of hitting the man instead of the tiger. In the midst of a whirlwind of dust and leaves, and a tempest of roars and yells, the bold native managed to drive his knife three times into the animal's side, when it rolled over with a savage growl and expired.

"Are ye hurt, Bunco?" inquired Will Osten with much anxiety, when the man rose, covered with dust and blood, and stood before them.

"No moche hurt, only scrash a bit."

"Scratched a bit!" exclaimed Larry, "it's torn to tatters ye ought to be for bein' so venturesome."

"That's so," said Muggins; "ye shouldn't ha' done it, Bunco; what would have comed of us if ye'd bin killed, eh?"

"Oh, dat am noting," said Bunco, drawing himself up proudly; "me hab kill lots of dem before; but dis one hims die hard."

Will Osten, who was anxious to ascertain whether the man had really escaped serious injury, put a stop to the conversation by hurrying him off to the nearest pool and washing his wounds. They proved, as he had said, to be trifling — only a slight bite on the shoulder and a few tears, by the animal's claws, on the arms and thighs. When these were dressed, Bunco went to work actively to skin the tiger, — an operation which he performed with great expedition, and then, having rolled it into a convenient bundle and slung it on his back, he re-loaded his gun and again resumed his duties as guide. They had not gone far when a fierce growling behind them told that other wild animals, probably tigers, had scented out the carcass of the slain animal, and were already quarrelling over their meal.

Shortly after this they came suddenly and quite unexpectedly on a house or hut, which turned out to be the residence of a man who was half Spaniard half Indian. The man received them kindly, and, finding that Bunco could speak Spanish, offered them hospitality with great politeness and evident satisfaction.

"Good luck to 'e, boy," said Larry, when their host invited them to partake of a substantial meal to which he had been about to sit down when they arrived, "it's myself'll be proud to welcome ye to ould Ireland if iver ye come that way."

"Ask him, Bunco," said Will Osten, "where we are, how far we are from the coast, and what is the name and distance of the nearest town."

To these questions the Spaniard replied that they were in the northern part of the Republic of Ecuador, and not, as they had supposed, in Peru, which lay some hundreds of miles to the southward; that a couple of days' walking would bring them to the coast, and that in two days more they could reach the town of Tacames. This, being one of the few ports on the western coast of South America where vessels touched, was a place from which they might probably be able to make their way to California. He added that there was a rumour of gold having been discovered of late in that region, but, for his part, he didn't believe it, for he had heard the same rumour several times before, and nothing had ever come of it, at least as far as he knew.

"Ye're wrong there, intirely, mister what's-yer-name," said Larry O'Hale, pausing for a moment in the midst of his devotion to the good things spread before him. "Sure it's my own brother Ted as wos out there a year gone by, an' he swore he picked up goold like stones an' putt them in his pocket, but the capting o' the ship he sailed in towld him it wos brass, an' his mates laughed at him to that extint that he flung it all overboord in a passion. Faix, I've made up my mind that there *is* goold in Callyforny and that wan Larry O'Hale is distined for to make his fortin' there — so I'll throuble ye for another hunk o' that pottimus, or wotiver ye call it. Prime prog it is, anyhow."

An earnest discussion here followed as to the probability of gold having been found in California and whether it was worth their while to try their fortune in that direction. During the course of the meal, the Spaniard incidentally mentioned that on the previous night a tiger had broken into his enclosure, and injured a bullock so badly that he had been obliged to kill it, and he had little doubt the same beast would pay him another visit that night.

This was good news to the travellers, all of whom were keen — though not all expert — sportsmen.

As evening had already set in, they begged to be allowed to rest for a little so as to be ready for the tiger when he came. Their host at once conducted them into a small room, where several hammocks were suspended from the walls. Into these they quickly jumped, and, in a few minutes, the concert played by their noses told a tale of sweet repose after a day of unusual toil.

For several hours they slept, and then the Spaniard awoke them with the information that the tiger was coming! Up they sprang, as a matter of course, and with considerable noise too, but Bunco soon impressed them with the necessity of being quiet. The Spaniard had only two guns, one of which he handed to Will Osten. The seamen were of necessity left to be spectators.

It is necessary here to describe the Spaniard's hut, which was peculiar as to its architecture. It was a mere shed made of bamboo canes closely placed together, and roofed with large cocoa and other leaves. The floor was of rough boards covered with matting. The whole structure stood on the top of a number of strong posts about twelve or fourteen feet from the ground, and the entrance was gained by a ladder which could be drawn up at night. The object of this great elevation and the ladder, was protection from the nocturnal visit of wild beasts such as tigers or jaguars, as well as monkeys of a large size. In the door of this hut there was a hole of about two feet square, at which the host stationed himself with the muzzle of his gun thrust through it. Two smaller holes in the walls, which served for windows, were used on the present occasion as loopholes by Will Osten and Bunco.

Perfect silence was maintained for about half an hour. The sky was cloudless and the moon full. Not a breath of wind stirred a leaf of the forest that encircled the small clearing. The buzz of mosquitoes, or the flapping about of a huge bat alone disturbed the silence of the night, and the watchers were beginning to fear it would turn out to be a false alarm, when the cattle in the yard began to low in a quick yet mournful tone. They knew full well that their enemy was at hand! A few minutes, that appeared an age, of anxiety followed. Then some bullocks that had been purposely fastened near the hut began to bellow furiously. Another instant, and the tiger cleared the fence with a magnificent bound, alighted in the yard, and crouched for a spring. The moon shone full in his glaring eyeballs, making his head a splendid target. Three shots crashed out in one report, and with a roar that would have done credit to the monarch of the African wilderness, this king of the western forest fell down and died.

He was a full-grown tiger with a beautifully marked skin, which Bunco was not long in stripping from the carcass, while the Spaniard, who was highly delighted by this success, set about preparing breakfast. They were all too much excited to think of going to bed again; and, besides, it was within an hour of daybreak.

During the morning Will Osten persuaded his host to give him one of his old guns in exchange for a beautiful silver-mounted hunting knife, which was the only article of value that he happened to possess. With this useful addition to their arms, the travellers resumed their journey shortly after dawn, being convoyed several miles on their way by their amiable host. They parted from him, finally, with much regret and many professions of gratitude and esteem, especially from Larry, who, in the fulness of his impulsive nature, reiterated his pressing invitation to pay him a visit in his "swait little cabin in the bog of Clonave, County Westmeath, ould Ireland!"

We will not drag the reader through every step of the rough and adventurous journey which was accomplished by our travellers in the succeeding week, during which they became so familiar with tigers, that Muggins thought no more of their roaring than he did of the mewing of cats, while Larry actually got the length of kicking the "sarpints" out of his way, although he did express his conviction, now and then, that the "counthry wos mightily in want of a visit from Saint Patrick." They travelled steadily and surely under the guidance of the faithful Bunco, through tangled brake, and wild morass, and dense forest, and many a mile of sandy plain, until at length they reached the small town and port of *Tacames*, into which they entered one sultry afternoon, footsore and weary, with their clothes torn almost to tatters, and without a single coin — of any realm whatever — in their pockets.

"Well, here we are at last," said Will Osten, with a sigh.

"True for ye," responded Larry.

"That's so," said Muggins.

"It's all well as ends well, which wos Billy Cowper's opinion," observed Old Peter.

Bunco made no remark, but he gave a quiet grunt, which might have meant anything — or nothing — as they entered the town.

CHAPTER IX.

Describes a Surgical Operation, and records the Deliberations of a Council.

The town of Tacames, in the republic of Ecuador, is not large, neither is it important to the world, but it appeared both large and important in the eyes of our hero and his comrades. In their circumstances any town would have been regarded as a city of refuge, and their joy on arriving was not much, if at all, marred by the smallness and the poor appearance of the town, which, at that time, consisted of about twenty houses. They were built on the top of posts about twelve or fourteen feet from the ground — like the hut of the Spaniard already described — because, being closely walled in by a dense jungle, tigers and huge monkeys were bold enough to pay the inhabitants nocturnal and unwelcome visits very frequently.

"A curious-looking place," observed Will Osten, as they drew near.

"So would the natives obsarve of London or Liverpool," said Old Peter.

"With less cause, however," replied Will.

"That depends on taste," retorted Old Peter.

"Be no manes," put in Larry; "it neither depinds on taste, nor smell, but feelin' — see now, here's how it is. We being in Tickamis, *feels* it coorious; well av the natives here wos in London *they* would feel it coorious. It's all a matter o' feelin' d'ye see — wan o' the five senses."

"Wot a muddlehead you are, Larry," growled Muggins; "ye don't even know that there's six senses."

"Only five," said the Irishman firmly — "seein', hearin', tastin', smellin', and feelin'; wot's the sixth sense?"

"One that you are chock full of — it's non-sense," replied Muggins.

"Think o' that, now!" exclaimed Larry, with a broad grin; "sure I wint an' forgot it, an' the sevinth wan, too, called common sense, of which, Muggins, you haven't got no more in yer skull than a blue-faced baboon. Hallo! wot's that? Is it a wild baist on its hind-legs or only a mad man?"

He pointed as he spoke to a man who approached them from the town, and whose appearance as well as his actions were well calculated to surprise them. He was a fine-looking man of gigantic size, with a poncho over his shoulders and a Spanish-looking sombrero on his head, but the most curious thing about him was his gait. At one moment he sauntered, holding his face between both hands, next moment he bent double and appeared to stamp with his feet. Then he hurried forward a few paces but paused abruptly, bent down and stamped again. Presently he caught sight of the travellers. At once his antics ceased. He raised himself erect, and advancing quickly, lifted his sombrero and saluted them with the air of a prince.

Will Osten addressed him in English, and, to his surprise as well as gratification, the Spaniard replied in the same tongue, which he spoke, however, in a most remarkable way, having learned it chiefly from the skippers of those vessels that touched at the port.

"I sall be happy to offer you hospitabilities, gentlemans," said Don Diego — (for so he styled himself). "If you vill come to meen house you vill grub there."

The grin of unnatural ferocity which Don Diego put on

while he spoke, surprised and perplexed the travellers not a little, but he suddenly explained the mystery by clutching his hair, setting his teeth and muttering wildly while he gave a quick stamp with his foot —

"Skuse me, gentlemans, I got most desperable 'tack of toothick!"

Will Osten attempted to console Don Diego by telling him that he was a surgeon, and that if he could only obtain a pair of pincers he would soon remedy that evil; but the Spaniard shook his head and assured him that there was a miserable man in the town calling himself a vendor of physic, who had already nearly driven him mad by attempting several times to pull the tooth, but in vain.

"Indeed," said the Don, "the last time he have try, I 'fraid I shut up won of his days light — it *was* so sore!"

Will Osten ultimately persuaded the Spaniard, however, to consent to an operation, and the whole party accompanied him to his house, which was the most substantial in the town. Leaving his comrades there, Will went with Bunco in search of the apothecary, whom he soon found, and who readily lent him a pair of forceps, with which he returned to the residence of Don Diego. Considering his size, Will deemed it advisable to have Larry and Muggins standing by ready to hold him if he should prove obstreperous. This was a wise precaution, for, the moment Will began to pull at the obstinate grinder, the gigantic Don began to roar and then to struggle. The tooth was terribly firm. Will did not wonder that the native dentist had failed. The first wrench had no effect on it. The second — a very powerful one — was equally futile, but it caused Don Diego to roar hideously and to kick, so Will gave a nod to his assistants, who unceremoniously seized the big man in their iron gripe and held him fast. Then our hero threw all his strength into a final effort, and the tooth came out with a crash, and, along with it, a terrible yell from Don Diego, who sent Larry and Muggins staggering against the wall! The relief experienced by the poor man was almost instantaneous; as soon as he could speak he thanked Will in fervid Spanish, and with genuine gratitude.

It is interesting to observe how often matters of apparently slight moment in human affairs form turning-points which lead to important results. The incident which we have just related caused Don Diego to entertain such kindly feelings towards Will Osten, that he not only invited him to stay at his house with his companions during their residence in Tacames, but insisted on his accepting a very large fee for the service he had rendered him. Of course this was not objected to in the circumstances, but a still better piece of good fortune than this befell the wanderers. Will found that a number of the inhabitants had been attacked with dysentery, and that the ignorance of the vendor of physic was so great, that he could do nothing for them, except make a few daring experiments, which were eminently unsuccessful. To these poor invalids our embryo doctor was so useful, that after a few days dosing with proper medicine, their health and spirits began to improve rapidly, and their gratitude was such that they heaped upon him every delicacy that the place afforded, such as bananas, plantains, oranges, lemons, pumpkins, melons, sweet potatoes, beef, goat's flesh, venison, and pork, besides filling his pockets with doubloons! Thus it came to pass, that from absolute destitution Will and his comrades suddenly leaped into a condition of comparative affluence.

At the end of a week a council was called, to discuss future proceedings. The council chamber was, as usual, the forest, and Spanish cigarettes assisted the deliberations. Will being called to the chair, which was a tree stump, opened the proceedings by propounding the question, "What shall we do now, for of course we must not trespass too long on the hospitality of Don Diego?"

"I don't see why we shudn't," said Larry, "p'raps he'll have another touch o' toothache, an' 'll want another grinder tuck out."

"That may be, nevertheless it behoves us to fix our future plans without delay. As there are no vessels in port just now, and we cannot tell when any will arrive, it is worth while considering whether we cannot travel by land; also, we must decide whether California or England is to be our destination."

"I vote for Callyforny," said Larry O'Hale with much energy. "'Goold for ever,' is my motto! Make our fortunes right off, go home, take villas in ould Ireland, an' kape our carriages, wid flunkeys an' maid-servants an' such like. Sure av we can't get by say, we can walk."

"If I had wings, which is wot I haven't," said Muggins, with slow precision of utterance, "I might fly over the Andes, likewise the Atlantic, to England, or if I had legs ten fathoms long I might walk to Callyforny; but, havin' only short legs, more used to the sea than to the land, I votes for stoppin' where we are for some time, an', p'raps, a sail will heave in sight an' take us off, d'ye see?"

"Ho!" exclaimed Bunco, with a nod of approval, "and wees kin go huntin' for amoosement in de meaninwhiles."

"It's my opinion, sir," observed Old Peter, "that as we're all dependent on the money earned by yourself, the least we can do is to leave you to settle the matter of when we start and where we go. What say you, mates?"

A general assent being given to this, Will Osten decided that they should remain where they were for a week or a fortnight longer, in the hope of a vessel arriving, and that, in the mean-time, as suggested by Bunco, they should amuse themselves by going on a hunting expedition.

In accordance with this plan they immediately set about making preparation for a start by borrowing from their host two small canoes, each made of the trunk of a large tree hollowed out. Bunco acted as steersman in one of these. Will Osten, after a few hours' practice, deemed himself sufficiently expert to take the post of honour in the other, and then, bidding adieu to Don Diego, and embarking with their guns and a large supply of ammunition and provisions, they commenced the ascent of the river Tacames, little thinking that some of the party would never descend that river or see Don Diego again!

CHAPTER X.

Hunting in the Wilds of Ecuador.

There is something very delightful and exhilarating in the first start on a hunting expedition into a wild and almost unknown region. After one gets into the thick of it the thoughts are usually too busy and too much in earnest with the actual realities in hand to permit of much rambling into the regions of romance — we say *much* because there is always *some* rambling of this sort — but, during the first day, before the actual work has well begun, while the adventures are as yet only anticipated, and the mind is free to revel in imaginings of what is possible and probable, there is a wild exultation which swells the heart and induces an irresistible tendency to shout. Indeed, on the present occasion, some of the party did shout lustily in order to vent their feelings; and Larry O'Hale, in particular, caused the jungle to echo so loudly with the sounds of his enthusiasm that the affrighted apes and jaguars must have trembled in their skins if they were possessed of ordinary feelings.

The scenery, with its accompaniments, was most beautiful and interesting. The river, a narrow one, flowed through a dense and continuous forest; rich and lofty trees over-arched it, affording agreeable shade, and on the branches were to be seen great numbers of kingfishers, parrots, and other birds of rich plumage, which filled the air at least with sound, if not with melody. The concert was further swelled by the constant cries of wild beasts — such as the howl of a tiger or the scream of a monkey. But there is no pleasure without some alloy. On this river mosquitoes were the alloy! These tormenting creatures persecuted the hunters by night as well as by day, for they are amongst the few insects which indulge in the pernicious habit of never going to bed. We cannot indeed say, authoritatively, that mosquitoes never sleep, but we can and do say that they torment human beings, and rob them of *their* sleep, if possible, without intermission. Larry O'Hale being of a fiery nature, was at first driven nearly to distraction, and, as he said himself, he did little else than slap his own face day and night in trying to kill "the little varmints." Muggins bore up stoically, and all of them became callous in course of time. Fish of many kinds were seen in the clear water, and their first success in the sporting way was the spearing of two fine mullet. Soon after this incident, a herd of brown deer were seen to rush out of the jungle and dash down an open glade, with noses up and antlers resting back on their necks. A shot from Bunco's gun alarmed but did not hit them, for Bunco had been taken by surprise, and was in an unstable canoe. Before the deer had disappeared, two or three loud roars were heard.

"Quick! go ashore," whispered Bunco, running his canoe in among the overhanging bushes, and jumping out.

Three tigers bounded at that moment from the jungle in pursuit of the deer. Bunco took rapid aim, but his old flint gun missed fire. Luckily, Will Osten, having followed his example, was ready. He fired, and one of the tigers fell, mortally wounded. Before he could wriggle into the jungle Bunco ran up and put a bullet into his brain.

This was a splendid beginning, and the hunters were loud in their congratulations of each other, while Bunco skinned the tiger. But the reader must not suppose that we intend to chronicle every incident of this kind. We record this as a specimen of their work during the following three weeks. They did not indeed shoot a tiger daily, but they bagged several within that period, besides a number of deer and other game. We must hasten, however, to tell of an event which put a sudden stop to our hero's hunting at that time, and resulted in the breaking-up of that hitherto united and harmonious party.

One evening, a little before sunset, they came upon a small clearing, in the midst of which was a little house erected, in the usual way, upon wooden legs. The hunters found, to their surprise, that it was inhabited by an Englishman named Gordon, who received them with great hospitality and evident pleasure. He lived almost alone, having only one negro man-servant, whose old mother performed the duties of housekeeper. Here they passed the night in pleasant intercourse with a man, who, besides being a countryman — and therefore full of interest about England, from which he heard regularly but at long intervals — was remarkably intelligent, and had travelled in almost every quarter of the globe. As to his motive for secluding himself in such a wild spot, they did not presume to inquire, and never found it out.

Next day they bade their host adieu, promising to make a point of spending another night in his house on their return. Our hunters had not gone far when a growl in one of the bushes induced them to land and search for the growler. They found him in the person of a large tiger, which Will Osten caught a glimpse of sneaking away with the lithe motions of a gigantic cat. A hurried shot wounded the beast, which, instead of flying, turned round suddenly, and, with a bound, alighted on our hero's shoulders. The shock hurled him violently to the ground. During the momentary but terrific struggle for life that followed, Will had presence of mind to draw his hunting-knife, and plunge it, twice, deep into the tiger's side, but the active claws of the creature tore his thighs and arms; several large blood-vessels were injured; the light faded from the eyes of Wandering Will; his strong arm lost its cunning, and, in the midst of a loud report, mingled with a roar like thunder in his ears, he fainted away.

When Will recovered his senses he found himself stretched on his back on a low couch in a hut, with a man kneeling over him, and his comrades gazing into his face with expressions of deep anxiety. Will attempted to speak, but could not; then he tried to move, and, in doing so, fainted. On recovering consciousness, he observed that no one was near him except Larry O'Hale, who lay extended at his side, looking through the open doorway of the hut, while a series of the most seraphic smiles played on his expressive countenance!

It would have been an interesting study to have watched the Irishman on that occasion. Just before Will Osten opened his eyes, he was looking into his pale face with an expression that was ludicrously woe-begone. The instant he observed the slightest motion in his patient, however, he became suddenly abstracted, and gazed, as we have said, with a seraphic expression through the doorway. Poor Larry acted thus, in order to avoid alarming his patient by his looks, but, in spite of his utmost caution, Will caught him in the transition state, which so tickled his risible faculties that he burst into a laugh, which only got the length of a sigh, however, and nearly produced another fainting fit.

"Ah, then, darlin'!" whispered Larry, with the tenderness of a woman, "*don't* do it now. Sure ye'll go off again av ye do. Kape quiet, dear. 'Tis all right ye'll be in a day or two. Bad luck to the baist that did it!"

This latter remark brought the scene of the tiger-hunt suddenly to Will's remembrance, and he whispered, for he had not strength to speak aloud —

"Was he killed? Who saved me?"

"Kilt!" cried Larry, forgetting his caution in his excitement;

"faix he was, an' Bunco did it, too — blissin's on his dirty face — putt the ball betune his two eyes an' took the laist bit of skin off yer own nose, but the blood was spoutin' from ye like wather, an' if it hadn't bin that the cliver feller knowed all about tyin' up an' — there, honey, I wint an' forgot — don't mind me — och! sure, he's off again!"

This was true. Our hero had lost almost the last drop of blood that he could spare with the slightest chance of recovery, and the mere exertion of listening was too much for him.

For many weeks he lay in the hut of that hospitable Englishman, slowly but gradually returning from the brink of the grave, and during this period he found his host to be a friend in need, not only to his torn and weak body, but also to his soul.

Day after day Gordon sat beside his couch with unwearied kindness, chatting to him about the "old country," telling him anecdotes of his former life, and gradually leading him to raise his thoughts from the consideration of time to eternity.

Will Osten, like every unconverted man, rebelled at this at first; but Gordon was not a man to be easily repulsed. He did not *force* religious thoughts on Will, but his own thoughts were so saturated, if we may say so, with religion, that he could not avoid the subject, and his spirit and manner were so winning that our hero was at last pleased to listen. Will's recovery was slow and tedious. Before he was able to leave Gordon's cottage his "independent" spirit was subdued by the Spirit of God, and he was enabled to exchange slavery to Self for freedom in the service of Jesus Christ. For many a day after that did Will Osten lie helpless on his couch, perusing with deep interest the Testament given to him by his mother when he left home.

During this period his companions did not forsake him, but spent their time in hunting and conveying the proceeds to Tacames, where they disposed of them profitably. On one of these occasions they found that an English ship had touched at the port in passing, and, among other things, Larry brought a number of old newspapers to the invalid. Among the first that he opened Will read the announcement of the sudden death of his own father! No information was given beyond the usual and formal statement, with the simple addition of the words "deeply regretted."

We need not say that this was a terrible shock to the poor wanderer — a shock which was rendered all the more severe when he reflected that he had parted from his father in anger. In his weak condition, Will could not bear up under the blow, and, for some days, he lay in such a depressed state of mind and body that his comrades began to fear for his life. But after that he rallied, and a sudden improvement took place in his health.

One day he called his companions round him, and said:

"Friends, I have resolved to leave you and return to Europe. You know my reasons. I am not a companion, but only a drag upon you; besides, my mother is left unprotected. You will excuse me if I decline to enter into a discussion on this point. I have not strength for it, and my resolve is fixed."

Will paused, and Larry O'Hale, with a leer on his countenance, asked by what road he meant to travel.

"Across the Andes to the northern coast of South America," answered Will, smiling.

"An' you as waik as wather, with legs like the pins of a wather-wagtail!"

"That will soon mend," said Will, jumping up and pulling on his clothes; "get ready to go out hunting with me, Larry, if you have a mind to!"

Despite the remonstrances of his friend, Will Osten went out with his gun, trembling with weakness at every step. He was soon induced to return to the cottage, but his resolve was fixed.

Next day he went out again, and, finally, in the course of a week or two, had recovered so much of his old vigour that he felt able to set out on his journey. Of course there were many disputings and arguings as to who should go with him, but it was finally agree that Larry and Bunco should be his companions. Indeed these two would take no denial, and vowed that if he declined to accept of them as comrades they would follow him as a rear-guard! Muggins and Old Peter decided that they would return to Tacames, and make their way thence to California.

Just before parting, Larry took Muggins aside and said, in as dismal a tone as his jovial spirit was capable of, "It's little I thought, mate, that you an' me would come for to part in this way, but ov coorse, I couldn't leave Mr. Osten in such a fix, so, d'ye see, I must say farewell; but kape yer weather eye open, ould boy, for as sure as Larry O'Hale has got two legs, which makes a pair, you'll see him in Callyforny yit, diggin' for his fortin'. In the main time, as I know ye'll want money, an' as I've made a lot more than you by huntin' — becase of being a better shot, d'ye see — here's a small sum which I axes you to accept of as a testimoniyall of my ondyin' friendship."

Muggins bluntly refused the leathern bag which Larry thrust into his hand, but he ultimately allowed him to force it into his pocket — and turned away with a sigh.

It was a lovely morning when Wandering Will sorrowfully bade his friends farewell, and, with his faithful followers, turned his face towards the snow-capped range of the mighty Andes.

CHAPTER XI.

Wandering Will travels, finds his Profession Profitable,
and sees a Good Deal of Life in New Forms.

The first part of the journey was performed in a canoe on the Tacames river, up which they ascended with considerable speed. The scenery was delightfully varied. In some places the stream was wide, in others very narrow, fringed along the banks with the most luxuriant timber and brushwood, in which the concert kept up by birds and beasts was constant but not disagreeable to the ears of such enthusiastic sportsmen as Will Osten, Larry O'Hale, and Bunco. The only disagreeable objects in the landscape were the alligators, which hideously ugly creatures were seen, covered with mud, crawling along the banks and over slimy places, with a sluggish motion of their bodies and an antediluvian sort of glare in their eyes that was peculiarly disgusting. They were found to be comparatively harmless, however. If they had chanced to catch a man asleep they would have seized him no doubt, and dragged him into the water, but being arrant cowards, they had not the pluck to face even a little boy when he was in motion.

Towards the afternoon of the first day, the hunters came to a long bend in the river. Here Will Osten resolved to leave Bunco to proceed alone with the canoe, while he and Larry crossed the country in search of game. Their friend Gordon had given them an elaborate chart of the route up to the mountains, so that they knew there was a narrow neck of jungle over which they might pass and meet the canoe after it had traversed the bend in the river.

"Have you got the tinder-box, Larry?" inquired Will, as they were about to start.

"Ay, an' the powder an' shot too, not to mintion the bowie-knife. Bad luck to the wild baists as comes to close quarters wid me, anyhow."

He displayed an enormous and glittering knife as he spoke, with which he made two or three savage cuts and thrusts at imaginary tigers before returning it to its sheath.

Cautioning Bunco to keep a good look-out for them on the other side of the neck of land, the hunters entered the forest. For several hours they trudged through bush and brake, over hill and dale, in jungle and morass, meadow and ravine, without seeing anything worth powder and shot, although they *heard* the cries of many wild creatures.

"Och! there's wan at long last," whispered Larry, on coming to the edge of a precipice that overlooked a gorge or hollow, at the bottom of which a tiger was seen tearing to pieces the carcase of a poor goat that it had captured. It was a long shot, but Larry was impatient. He raised his gun, fired, and missed. Will Osten fired immediately and wounded the brute, which limped away, howling, and escaped. The carcass of the goat, however, re-mained, so the hunters cut off the best parts of the flesh for supper, and then hastened to rejoin the canoe, for the shades of night were beginning to fall. For an hour longer they walked, and then suddenly they both stopped and looked at each other.

"I do belaive we've gone an' lost ourselves again," said Larry.

"I am afraid you are right," replied Will, with a half smile; "come, try to climb to the top of yonder tree on the eminence; perhaps you may be able to see from it how the land lies."

Larry went off at once, but on coming down said it was so

dark that he could see nothing but dense forest everywhere. There was nothing for it now but to encamp in the woods. Selecting, therefore, a large spreading tree, Larry kindled a fire under it, and his companion in trouble discharged several shots in succession to let Bunco know their position if he should be within hearing.

Neither Will nor Larry took troubles of this kind much to heart. As soon as a roaring fire was blazing, with the sparks flying in clouds into the trees overhead, and the savoury smell of roasting goat's flesh perfuming the air, they threw care to the dogs and gave themselves up to the enjoyment of the hour, feeling assured that Bunco would never desert them, and that all should be well on the morrow. After supper they ascended the tree, for the howling of wild beasts increased as the night advanced, warning them that it would be dangerous to sleep on the ground. Here they made a sort of stage or platform among the branches, which was converted into a comfortable couch by being strewn six inches deep with leaves. Only one at a time dared venture to sleep, however, for creatures that could climb had to be guarded against. At first this was a light duty, but as time passed by it became extremely irksome, and when Larry was awakened by Will to take his second spell of watching, he vented his regrets in innumerable grunts, growls, coughs, and gasps, while he endeavoured to rub his eyes open with his knuckles.

"Have a care, lad," said Will, with a sleepy laugh as he lay down; "the tigers will mistake your noise for an invitation to —"

A snore terminated the speech.

"Bad luck to them," yawned Larry, endeavouring to gaze round him. In less than a minute his chin fell forward on his breast, and he began to tumble backwards. Awaking with a start under the impression that he was falling off the tree, he threw out both his arms violently and recovered himself.

"Come, Larry," he muttered to himself, with a facetious

smile of the most idiotical description, "don't give way like that, boy. Ain't ye standin' sintry? an' it's death by law to slaip at yer post. Och! but the eyes o' me won't kape open. Lean yer back agin that branch to kape ye from fallin'. There — now howld up like a man — like a — man — ould — b-o-oy." His words came slower and slower, until, at the last, his head dropped forward on his chest, and he fell into a profound sleep, to the immense delight of a very small monkey which had been watching his motions for some time, and which now ventured to approach and touch the various articles that lay beside the sleepers, with intense alarm, yet with fiendish glee, depicted on its small visage.

Thus some hours of the night were passed, but before morning the rest of the sleepers was rudely broken by one of the most appalling roars they had yet heard. They were up and wide awake instantly, with their guns ready and fingers on the triggers!

"It's draimin' we must have —"

A rustling in the branches overhead checked him, and next moment the roar was repeated. Larry, with an irresistible feeling of alarm, echoed it and fired right above his head — doing nothing more serious, however, than accelerating the flight of the already horrified monkey. The shot was followed by another roar, which ended in something like a hideous laugh.

"Sure 'tis a hieena!" exclaimed Larry, reloading in violent haste.

"A hyena!" exclaimed Will — "ay, and a black one, too! Come down, Bunco, you scoundrel, else I'll put a bullet in your thick skull."

At this invocation the rustling overhead increased, and Bunco dropped upon the platform, grinning from ear to ear at the success of his practical joke.

"Och, ye blackymoor!" cried Larry, seizing the native by the throat and shaking him; "what d'ye main be such doin's, eh?"

"Me mean noting," said Bunco, still chuckling prodigiously; "but it am most glorus fun for fright de bowld Irishesman."

"Sit down, ye kangaroo, an' tell us how ye found us out," cried Larry.

"You heard our shots, I suppose?" said Will. To this Bunco replied that he had not only heard their shots, but had seen them light their fire, and eat their supper, and prepare their couch, and go to sleep, all of which he enjoyed so intensely, in prospect of the joke he meant to perpetrate, that he was obliged to retire several times during the evening to a convenient distance and roar in imitation of a tiger, merely to relieve his feelings without betraying his presence. He added, that the canoe was about five minutes' walk from where they sat, and somewhat mollified the indignation of his comrades by saying that he would watch during the remainder of the night while they slept.

Next morning at daybreak the party re-embarked in the canoe and continued their journey. Soon the character of the country changed. After a few days the thick forests had disappeared, and richly cultivated small farms took their place. Everywhere they were most hospitably entertained by the inhabitants, who styled Will "Physico," because Bunco made a point of introducing him as a doctor. One evening they arrived at a little town with a small and rapid stream of water passing through it. There was a square in the centre of the town, surrounded by orange, lemon, and other trees, which formed an agreeable shade and filled the air with fragrance. Not only was there no doctor here, but one was seldom or never seen. Immediately, therefore, our Physico was besieged for advice, and his lancet, in particular, was in great request, for the community appeared to imagine that bloodletting was a cure for all the ills that flesh is heir to! Will of course did his best for them, and was surprised as well as pleased by the number of doubloons with which the grateful people fed him. After passing some days very pleasantly here, Will made preparations to continue his journey, when an express arrived bringing intelligence from several of the surrounding towns to the effect that a sort of revolution had broken out. It was fomented by a certain colonel in the employment of the State, who, finding that his services and those of his followers were not paid with sufficient regularity, took the simple method of recruiting his finances by a levy on the various towns in his neighbourhood. He was, in fact, a bandit. Some towns submitted, others remonstrated, and a few resisted. When it was ascertained that the colonel and his men were on their way to the town in which our travellers sojourned, preparations were at once made for defence, and of course Will Osten and his comrades could do no less than volunteer their services.

CHAPTER XII.

In which Terrible Things are treated of — The Andes are crossed, the Orinoco descended and the Book ended.

At the time of which we write it was not an uncommon thing, in the provinces on the western coast of South America, for dissatisfied military officers, with a number of malcontents, to get up miniature revolutions, which were generally put down after much plundering and bloodshed. These bands of armed men went about like regular banditti, disturbing the peace of the whole country. They were not much heard of in Europe, because intercommunication and telegraphy did not exist then as they do now, and insignificant affairs of the kind were not taken much notice of.

One effect of the threatened attack on the town about which we write was, that the people became desperately excited and tremendously vigorous in their preparations. Arms were sought out and distributed; chests were opened, and gold and silver — in quantities that amazed Will and his friends — taken out and buried in the woods. Pistols, guns, and swords were produced in abundance, with plenty of ammunition, and the manner in which the men handled these proved that they meant to make a determined stand. Trees were felled, and the roads leading to the town barricaded. As the express came along he spread the news around, and farmers came in from all quarters driving their cattle before them. All the arrangements for defence were made under the direction of Don Pedro, a retired officer, who proved to be quite equal to the occasion, posted his men judiciously, and sent out scouts on horseback. Will Osten, Larry, and Bunco were left to do as they pleased, so they armed themselves, procured horses, kept close together, and rode about the town observing the arrangements. The night passed without alarm, but early in the morning a horseman arrived with the news that the rebels were advancing. A few hours afterwards they appeared in full view. Some were mounted, but the majority were on foot, and a more villainous set of rascals could not well be imagined. They advanced irregularly, evidently not expecting opposition from so insignificant a town, but those who first approached the barricades were received with such a galling fire that several were killed, many wounded, and the rest driven back.

Their leader, a tall dark man on a powerful charger, rode to the front in a towering passion, and endeavoured to rally the men. At that moment a bold idea flashed upon Will Osten. He suddenly put spurs to his horse, galloped round to the lowest part of the barricade, leaped over it, and, drawing his sword, charged the leader of the rebels like a thunderbolt. The man faced him, and raised his sword, to defend himself, but Will's first cut was so powerful that it broke down his guard, cleft his helmet, and tumbled him out of the saddle.

The contending parties had scarce time to realise what was being done when the deed was completed, and a wild cheer burst from the townspeople, high above which there sounded a terrific "hooroo!" and next instant, Larry O'Hale, followed by Bunco, shot from the barricades, and charged the foe! The consternation caused by the suddenness and the unexpected nature of this onset made the banditti waver, and, when they beheld the townsmen pouring out from their defences and rushing at them with an evident determination to conquer or die, they turned and fled! The rout was complete, and for some time the people of the town continued to chase and slay the enemy, until the pursuit was suddenly stopped by an event as terrible as it was unexpected.

For some weeks previous to the day when the town was assaulted, the neighbourhood, and, indeed, the whole of the surrounding provinces, had been visited by a series of slight earthquakes. So common are these tremblings and heavings of the earth in South America, that unless very severe, not much notice is taken of them. At the time of which we write, the slight shocks had been so frequent that the people were comparatively indifferent to them. On the very day of the assault there had been several smarter shocks than usual, and some of the more thoughtful among the inhabitants remembered that it was on an unusually dry summer, similar to the one that was then passing, that a terrible earthquake had visited the province of Venezuela and entirely demolished the city of Caraccas. But the sudden attack of the rebels had for the time banished all thought of earthquakes.

It was while the people of the town were pursuing their enemies that another shock of the earthquake occurred, and it was so violent that many of the pursuers paused, while others turned at once and ran back to the town. Here they found the women and children in a state of consternation, for they had more thoroughly realised the force of the shock; and the dreadful scenes that had taken place in Caraccas, when upwards of ten thousand of the inhabitants perished, were still fresh in their memory. Another shock occurred just as Don Pedro, Will Osten, and his friends galloped into the principal square of the town. Here there were hundreds of cattle which had been driven there for safety, and crowds of people hurrying to and fro. The horsemen rode towards the principal church of the town, which had been made a place of temporary retreat for the women and children. They had got within a few hundred yards of it when there came a shock so terrible that it seemed as if the binding forces of nature were being dissolved. Hollow thunderings were heard deep in the bowels of the earth, which heaved and undulated almost as if it had been in a semi-liquid state, while great rents and fissures occurred here and there. Will Osten's horse stumbled into one of these and threw him, but he leaped up unhurt. Don Pedro and the others pulled up and dismounted hastily. Before they could make up their minds which way to turn or what to do, another shock occurred; the houses on either side of them began to sway to and fro, and one not far distant fell. Just then a terrible crash was heard, and Will Osten turned round in time to see the large church in the act of falling. Women and children were rushing out of it frantically, but those within were doomed. One wild and awful shriek mingled with the roar of the tumbling edifice, and five hundred souls were instantaneously buried in a common grave.

Terrible though this event was, much of the impression it was fitted to make on those who witnessed it was lost because of the danger that surrounded themselves. The shock or series of shocks continued for several minutes, during which time the houses were falling into ruins in all directions, and there was so much danger in remaining in any of the streets that most of the inhabitants who had escaped flocked, as with one consent, into the great square — many of them, however, being killed by falling masonry on their way thither. Others nearer the outskirts of the town fled into the woods.

When this shock ceased, the earthquake appeared to have terminated for that time, but even if it had continued, further damage could scarcely have been done, for the little town was reduced to a heap of ruins. The desolation was complete. Scarcely a house was left uninjured, and the greater part of the buildings were completely demolished. But the sights that met the eye were not more terrible than the sounds which filled the ear. Death and destruction reigned on every side. Groans of agony and frantic cries for deliverance were heard issuing from beneath the ruins, while men, women, and children were seen rushing about with dishevelled hair and bloodshot eyes, wildly searching for, and shouting the names of, their lost relatives and friends, or crying to God for mercy. It was a sickening and terrible sight — a sight in regard to which those who dwell in the more favoured parts of our sin-smitten world can form but a very faint conception.

At first all was disorder, but by degrees the spirits of the survivors began to calm down a little, and then systematic efforts were made to rescue those who had not been killed outright. It need scarcely be said that in this work our hero and his companions were conspicuously energetic. Will and Don Pedro organised the men into gangs and wherever cries or groans were heard, they tore up and removed the ruins so vigorously that the poor sufferers were speedily released; but in performing this work they uncovered the torn, crushed, and mangled bodies of hundreds of the dead.

"Come here, Larry," said Will, in a low, sad tone, as he stood on a pile of rubbish digging towards a spot where he had heard a faint cry as if from a female. The Irishman leaped to his side and saw a small hand sticking out of the rubbish. It quivered convulsively, showing that life still remained. With desperate eagerness, yet tender care, the two men disentombed the poor creature, who proved to be a women with a child clasped tightly in her broken and lacerated right arm. The woman was alive, but the poor child was dead, the skull having been completely smashed and its brains scattered on its mother's bosom. As they carried them away, the woman also expired.

In the course of a few hours great numbers of wounded persons, young and old, were laid under the lemon-trees by the banks of the little stream that traversed the town. Some were slightly hurt, but by far the greater number were terribly crushed and lacerated – many of them past all hope of recovery. To these sufferers Will Osten now gave his undivided attention, washing and bandaging wounds, amputating limbs, and endeavouring by every means to relieve them and save their lives, while to the dying he tried, in the little Spanish he knew, to convey words of spiritual comfort, sometimes finding it impossible to do more than whisper the name of Jesus in a dying ear, while hurriedly passing from one to another. If earnest heart-expressive glances from eyes that were slowly fading conveyed any evidence of good having been done, Will's labour of love was not spent in vain.

Reader, a volume would not suffice to detail a tithe of the sights and scenes of thrilling and dreadful interest that occurred in that small South American town on the occasion of the earthquake. Yet, awful though these were, they were as nothing compared with the more stupendous calamities that have been caused by earthquakes in that land of instability, not only in times long past, but in times so very recent that the moss cannot yet have begun to cover, nor the weather to stain, the tombstones and monuments of those who perished.

For many weeks Will Osten remained there tending the sick and dying. Then he bade his kind unfortunate friends farewell, and, once more turning his face towards the Cordillera of the Andes, resumed his homeward journey with his faithful attendants.

There are times in the career of a man – especially of one who leads a wandering and adventurous life – when it seems as though the events of a lifetime were compressed into the period of a few months, or weeks, or even days. Such, at least, was the experience of our hero while he travelled in the equatorial regions of South America. Events succeeded each other with such rapidity, and accumulated on each other to such an extent, that when he looked back it appeared utterly incredible that he and his companions had landed on the coast of Peru only a few months before. It was natural, indeed, that in such a region, where the phenomena and the forces of nature are so wild and vast, one incident or adventure should follow quickly on the heels of another, but it did not seem to be altogether natural that each incident should be more singular or tremendous than its predecessor. In short, there seemed to be neither rhyme nor reason, as Larry said, in the fact that they should be continually getting out of the frying-pan into the fire. Yet so it was, and, now that they had left the low country and plunged into the magnificent recesses of the great Andes, the metaphor was still applicable, though not, perhaps, equally appropriate, for, whereas the valleys they had quitted were sweltering in tropical heat, the mountains they had now ascended were clothed in wintry snow.

Far down in the valleys Will Osten and his friends had left their canoe, and hired mules with an *arriero* or mule-driver to guide them over the difficult and somewhat dangerous passes of the Andes. They had reached the higher altitudes of the mountains when we again introduce them to the reader, and were urging their mules forward, in order to reach a somewhat noted pass, before the breaking out of a storm which the arriero knew, from certain indications in the sky, was rapidly approaching. The party consisted of four — Will, Larry, Bunco, and the arriero — with three baggage-mules.

On reaching an elevated position at a turn in the road whence they could see far in advance, they halted.

"Why, I had supposed *this* was the pass," said Will Osten, turning to Bunco; "ask the arriero how far off it is now."

"Troth, it's my belaif that there's no pass at all," said Larry, somewhat doggedly, as he shifted about uneasily in the saddle;

"haven't we bin comin' up to places all day that we thought was the pass, — but they wasn't; I don't think Mister Arryhairo knows it hisself, and this baist of a mule has blistered my hands an' a'most broke my arms with baitin' of it — not to mintion other parts o' me body. Och, but it's a grand place, afther all — very nigh as purty as the Lakes of Killarney, only a bit bigger."

The country was indeed a little bigger! From the dizzy ledge on which they stood a scene of the wildest sublimity met their gaze, and, for a few minutes, the travellers regarded it in profound silence. Mountains, crags, gorges, snowy peaks, dark ravines, surrounded them, spread out below them, rose up above them everywhere in the utmost confusion. It was the perfection of desolation — the realisation of chaos. At their feet, far down in the gorge below, lay a lake so dark that it might have been ink; but it was clear and so very still that every rock in the cliffs around it was faithfully portrayed. High overhead rose one of the more elevated peaks of the Andes, which, being clothed in pure snow, looked airy — almost unreal — against the blue sky. The highest peak of the Andes (Chimborazo) is more than 21,000 feet above the sea. The one before them was probably a few hundred feet lower. Of living creatures, besides themselves, only one species was to be seen — the gigantic "condor" — the royal eagle of the Andes, which soars higher, it is said, than any other bird of its kind. Hundreds of condors were seen hovering above them, watching for their prey, — the worn-out and forsaken mules or cattle, which, while being driven over the pass, perished from exhaustion.

"The ugly brutes! Is it a goat they've got howld of there?" said Larry, pointing to a place where several of these monstrous eagles were apparently disputing about some prize.

On reaching the place, the object in question was found to be the skeleton of a mule, from which every morsel of flesh had been carefully picked.

"Hold my mule, Larry," whispered Will, throwing the reins to his comrade, and grasping a rifle with which one of his grateful patients who survived the earthquake had presented him. A condor had seated himself, in fancied security, on a cliff about two hundred yards off, but a well-aimed bullet brought him tumbling down. He was only winged, and when Will came up and saw his tremendous talons and beak, he paused to consider how he should lay hold of him.

"Och, what claws!" exclaimed Larry.

"Ah!" said Bunco, smiling, "more teribuble for scratch than yoos grandmoder, eh?"

Before they could decide how to proceed, the arriero came up, threw the noose of his lasso over the head of the magnificent bird, and secured it easily. He measured eight feet seven inches from tip to tip of the expanded wings.

Will Osten was anxious to skin this bird, and carry it away with him as a trophy, but the guide protested. He said that the pass was now really within a short distance of them, but that the thunder-storm would soon come on, and if it caught them in the pass they ran a chance of all being lost. Will, therefore, contented himself with cutting off the head and talons of the condor, and then resumed his toilsome upward journey.

According to the arriero's prophecy, the storm burst upon them in less than two hours, while they were still some distance from the top of the pass.

Although they had now reached the region of snow, the zigzag track by which they ascended was tolerably visible, but as they proceeded dark clouds overspread the sky, and snow fell heavily, while peals of muttering thunder came from afar, echoing among the mountain peaks and betokening the rapid approach of the storm. The arriero looked anxious, and urged the mules on with whip and voice, turning his eyes furtively, now and then, in the direction of the dark clouds. Presently, on turning one of the bends in the track, they came upon a singular party travelling in the opposite direction. Their singularity consisted chiefly in this, that instead of mules they had a train of bullock-waggons, which were laden with ponderous mill-machinery. At their head rode a fine-looking man of middle age, who addressed Will in Spanish. Bunco's services as interpreter being called into requisition, the traveller told them that the pass was pretty clear, but advised them to make haste, as the storm would soon break, and might render it impassable. On the same ground he excused himself for not staying to exchange news with them.

"Your cargo is a strange one," said Will, as they were about to part.

The traveller admitted that it was, and explained that he meant to erect a flour-mill in his native town, towards which he was hastening.

At these words the arriero seemed peculiarly affected. He advanced to the traveller and said a few words. The latter started, turned pale, and asked a few hurried questions. While the arriero was replying, the pallor of the traveller's countenance increased; a wild fire seemed to shoot from his eyes, and his hands clutched convulsively the poncho which covered his breast. Suddenly he returned to his followers and gave them a few hurried orders, then, without noticing any one, he put spurs to his mule, and galloping down the track like a madman, was out of sight in a moment. His men at once unharnessed the cattle and followed him, leaving the waggons and the ponderous machinery in the snow.

The first gust of the storm burst upon the travellers at this moment, and Will with his friends had to ride to a neighbouring cliff for shelter before he could ask the meaning of the peculiar conduct of the stranger. The guide soon cleared up the mystery by telling him, through Bunco, that the traveller was an inhabitant of the town which had been so recently destroyed by the earthquake. "I happened to know him by name," continued the guide, "and am aware that his wife with every member of his family was buried in the ruins. You saw how deeply he took it to heart, poor fellow."

"Poor fellow indeed; God help him," said Will sadly, as he left the shelter of the cliff, and continued the ascent.

They never saw the unfortunate man again, but it is worthy of remark that, years after, Will Osten heard of him through a friend who happened to cross the Andes at the same point. The blow had been so severe that he never returned to claim his property; and there it lay for many a day on the wild mountain pass — perchance there it lies still — far from the abodes of men, and utterly useless, save as a ponderous monument and memorial of the terrible catastrophe which had robbed its owner of home, kindred, wealth, and earthly hope.

The storm had at last burst upon our travellers in all its fury — and very different is the storm in these weird altitudes, where earth and heaven seem to meet, than in the plains below. The wind came whistling down the gorges as if through funnels, driving before it not only snow, but sand and pebbles, so that for a time our travellers being unable to face it, were compelled to seek shelter under a ledge of rock. After the first burst there was a short lull, of which they availed themselves to push on. Will, being mounted on the best mule, went considerably ahead of his companions; but at last the falling snow became so thick as to render objects almost invisible. The track, too, which ran unpleasantly near the edge of a precipice, was almost obliterated, so he thought it best to wait for the others. Just then another squall came howling down the gorge at his right. His mule became restive and frightened, and, slipping on the snow, came down on its knees. The violence of the wind rendered it almost impossible to keep the saddle, so this decided Will. He slid off. Scarcely had he done so when there came a gust which fortunately threw him flat down; at the same time his mule staggered over the edge of the precipice. One moment Will saw the poor animal struggling to regain its footing — the next it was rolling down into the abyss, bounding from rock to rock, and he knew, although the swirling snow prevented him seeing it, that his steed was, in a few minutes, dashed to pieces in the gorge a thousand feet below. For some time Will did not dare to rise. The gale grew fiercer every moment, and the darkness — not of night, but of thick clouds — increased. As the snow accumulated over him he feared being buried alive, so he struggled out of the drift and looked around him. It was utter chaos — not a landmark was visible. Having turned round once or twice, he did not know how to direct his steps. While hesitating as to what he should do, another gust swept by, carried away his hat and poncho, tore his over-coat right up the back and compelled him to lie down again, in which position he remained until he felt benumbed with cold. Knowing that to remain much longer in that position would insure his death, our hero rose and staggered forward a few paces — he scarce knew whither. There was a lull in the gale at this time, and he continued to advance, when a voice behind arrested him.

"Hooroo! doctor, whereabouts are ye?"

"Hallo! Larry, here I am, all right."

"Faix, it's well ye are that same," said Larry, looming through the drifting snow like a white spectre, "for it's all wrong with us. Wan o' the poor baists wi' the packs has gone clane over the cliffs an' bin smashed to smithereens — more be token it's the wan that carried the kittle an' the salt beef, but the wan wi' the biscuit an' the fryin'-pan is safe, an' that's a comfort, anyhow."

Will expressed his regret at this, and was beginning to tell how his own mule had been killed, when Bunco suddenly made his appearance, and, seizing him by the collar, dragged him with extreme violence a few paces forward. For one brief instant a flush of anger mingled with Will's surprise at this unceremonious treatment; but all other feelings gave way to one of gratitude to God when, observing his faithful attendant point to the spot from which he had been dragged, he turned round and saw that he had been standing on the extreme verge of the precipice. Had he advanced one step after being arrested by the voice of his comrade, his mangled body would, in a few seconds, have been lying beside that of his poor mule!

There was no time to speak of these things, however, just then, for the storm, or rather the squall, burst forth again with increased violence, and the pass was still before them — so like the men of a forlorn hope who press up to the breach, they braced themselves to renew the conflict, and pushed on. The truth of the proverb, that "fortune favours the brave," was verified on this occasion. The storm passed over almost as quickly as it had begun, the sky cleared up, and, before night set in, they had crossed the pass, and were rapidly descending the eastern side of the mountains towards the fertile plains and valleys of Columbia.

The transition from the wintry cold of the high regions of the Andes to the intense tropical heat of the plains and forests was rapidly made. In a few days the travellers were obliged to throw off their ponchos and warm garments, and at the end of a few weeks we find them stretched out lazily in the stern of a canoe, under the guidance of four Creoles, floating quietly down one of the numerous tributaries of the Orinoco. The change was not only sudden but also agreeable. In truth, our adventurers had been so long subjected by that time to excitement and exhausting toil — especially while crossing the mountains — that the most robust among them began to long for a little rest, both bodily and mental, and, now that they lay idly on their backs gazing at the passing scenery, listening to the ripple of the water and smoking cigarettes, it seemed as if the troubles of life had all passed away and nothing but peace lay around and before them.

"'Tis paradise intirely," observed Larry, removing his cigarette for a moment, and winking facetiously at a small monkey which happened to peep at him just then through the foliage overhead.

"Him won't be long like dat," said Bunco.

"Come, now, ye ill-omened spalpeen, don't be causin' yer dirty clouds to come over this purty vision. Wot's the use o' cryin' before ye're hurt, or pretendin' to know the futur' whin ye knows nothin' about it? Ye're no better than a baboon, Bunco, as I've fraiquintly had occasion to tell ye before now."

Bunco made no reply to this, but smiled slightly as he changed his position to one of greater comfort, and lit a fresh cigarette.

"Larry," said Will Osten, "did you remember to put the fresh meat in the canoe this morning?"

"Och! morther," cried the Irishman, starting up with a look of desperate annoyance on his expressive face; "sure I've wint an' forgot it! It's hangin' at this minit on the branch where I putt it last night for fear o' the tigers — bad luck to them!"

"Ho, ho!" ejaculated Bunco, "paradise am gone a'ready!"

Larry turned upon his friend with a look that betokened no good, and appeared to meditate an assault, when Will Osten said quietly, — "Never mind, Larry; I luckily observed your omission, and put it into the canoe myself."

"Ah, then, doctor, it's not right of 'e to trifle wid a poor man's feelin's in that way, especially in regard to his stummick, which, wid me, is a tinder point. Howsever, it's all right, so I'll light another o' thim cigarettes. They're not bad things after all, though small an' waik at the best for a man as was used to twist an' a black pipe since he was two foot high."

The Irishman lay down and once more sought to recover his lost paradise, but was interrupted by an exclamation from one of the canoe-men, who pointed to a part of the river's bank where no fewer than eight crocodiles were lying basking in the sun. They were of various sizes, from eight to twenty feet in length, and slept with their jaws wide open, and their formidable rows of teeth exposed to view.

"Well, wot's to do?" asked Larry, half rising.

"Oh! hums only want you to look to de brutes — 'tink you hab never seed him 'fore to-day," said Bunco.

"Tell him he's mistaken, then," replied Larry testily; "we've often seed 'em before, an' don't want to be roused up by such tri-fles."

Saying this, the Irishman once more sank into a recumbent state of felicity; but his peaceful tendency was doomed to fre-quent interruptions, not only on that day, but on many other occasions during the voyage down the Orinoco.

In the evening of that same day he had an adventure which induced him to suspect, more strongly even than Bunco, that ter-restrial paradise was indeed still a long way off. The party landed at a small clearing, where they were hospitably received by a pro-fessional tiger-hunter, who, although nearly half-naked and almost black, was a very dignified personage, and called himself Don Emanuel. This Don invited them up to smoke and eat at his residence, which turned out to be a very large one — no less than the wild forest itself, for he disdained houses, and was wont to sling his hammock, nightly, between two trees. At his encamp-ment they were introduced to his wife and two daughters, who were as wild and as lightly clad as himself, and the only evidence (if evidence it was) that the ladies belonged to the gentler sex was, that Donna Isabella — the elder sister — fondled a large cat, for which she appeared to entertain a strong affection. Having supped and smoked, the travellers slung their hammocks to the trees and went to sleep. In the middle of the night, several times, they were awakened by the cries of the denizens of the thickets. It was supposed that when any two of these took to fighting the others were stirred up to roar in sympathy! Be this as it may, the mingled cries, roars, and shrieks, of sapajous, alouates, jaguars, cougars, pacaris, sloths, curassows, parraquas, etc., broke forth from time to time with such fury, that sleep was almost unattainable; then a thunderstorm came on which wet them to the skin; after that a large vampire-bat bit Bunco on the nose, causing that worthy to add his noise to the general concert; and, finally, a soft hairy animal dropt from a branch into Larry O'Hale's hammock. The Irishman received it with open arms and a yell of terror. He crushed it to his chest, which drew forth a responsive yell of agony from the animal, whose claws and teeth were instantly fixed in Larry's chin and cheeks. He caught it by the tail — the teeth and claws were at once transferred to his hands; then he seized it by the throat, from which there issued a gasping shriek as he hurled it high into the air, whence it descended into the embers of the expiring fire, and, bolting violently from that too-warm spot, sent up a shower of sparks which revealed the fact that the unfortunate man had all but annihilated Donna Isabella's favourite cat!

Thus they proceeded down the Orinoco, and, finally, reached the sea-coast, where they opportunely found a vessel ready to sail for Old England. It was not long, therefore, before they were once more out upon the wide sea, with the happy consciousness that they were actually "homeward bound."

There are times in a man's career when realities appear to memory like the dim shadows of a dream, just as there are periods when dreams rise up with all the bold and startling vividness of reality. Our adventurers felt something of this when they had been a few days at sea, and began to think of and talk about their recent career in South America. It seemed to them as though their romantic life in the woods, their encounters with wild beasts, their adventures and misadventures in Ecuador, their dangers and difficulties in crossing the Andes, and their tranquil descent of the Orinoco, were a confused yet vivid vision; and often, while pacing the deck together, or sitting on the bulwarks of the ship in the dreamy idleness of passenger-life at sea, did they comment upon the difficulty they had in regarding as indubitable facts the events of the last few months.

Nevertheless, as Larry expressed it, there could be no doubt whatever that it was all true, and after all, according to his carefully formed estimate, worse luck might have befallen them than being "cast away on the shores of Peroo an' lost in the forest!"

www.ingramcontent.com/pod-product-compliance
Lightning Source LLC
Chambersburg PA
CBHW022047170626
46808CB00003B/1383